Magicians & Murder

A Paranormal Witch Cozy Witch Mystery

Book Store Cozy Mystery Series
Book 7

Lucinda Race

MC Two Press

1. Robin's Cafe
2. Bygone Antiques
3. The Pembroke Cliffs
4. Cozy Nook Bookstore
5. Twisted Scissors Hair Salon
6. Betty's Market
7. Old Town Libary
8. Miss Judy's Dance Studio
9. The Sweet Spot Baker
10. Bee Bee's Boutique
11. Tuckers Hardware Store
12. The Copper Kettle
13. Police Station
14. Town Hall

Chapter 1
Lily

QUICK NOTE: If you enjoy Magicians & Murder, be sure to check out my offer for a FREE novella at the end. With that, happy reading.

I looked at my watch for the third time and decided to make a pot of coffee. Wandering into the tiny kitchen that doubled as the storage room in the back of my bookstore, I cast a quick but effective spell to start the coffee brewing. I stepped into the main room and looked out the front windows overlooking Main Street. The calendar said it was April, but today the blowing flakes of snow reminded me winter still had a firm grip on the tiny town of Pembroke Cove. And still no Nikki.

My best friend had been on her honeymoon, and I was anxious to hear all about it. I blushed as I rephrased that in my head—about the vacation part, restaurants, and what they did. In turn, I was going to fill her in on the details of the case about poor John Bailey, the treasure hunter running around town dressed as a leprechaun, and the cause of his untimely death.

I looked at Milo, my gray tabby cat and familiar, soaking up the morning sun on the wide windowsill. The smile on my face changed from friend zone to business person in the blink of an eye. Standing outside the store were two couples. The women were tall and willowy and looked like they stepped from the pages of a fashion magazine. The older gentleman had piercing blue eyes, dark hair with strands of silver, high cheekbones, and a long, thin nose. He was *stop in your tracks* handsome, and next to him was the fourth person, who also was dipped in the gorgeous gene pool. He looked similar to the tall man, but younger, with blond hair and deep brown eyes. The small bell above the front door jingled as they entered.

"Welcome to the Cozy Nook Bookshop." I swept my hand from side to side. "Browse to your heart's content, and if you're looking for something specific, be sure to let me know. We have an extensive section on local history and authors in aisle one."

"Thank you." The woman with auburn hair turned to the brunette and said, "We should start there."

I took a step closer, but my pulse ticked up. Animosity wrapped around them like a cloak, and I didn't go any farther. I wished Milo would saunter by the desk. He'd get a good read on them in half a minute or less. The older man looked me up and down.

"Do you work here?" His voice was deep and rich but cold and harsh at the same time, which made no sense to me at all. It was so conflicting.

"I'm the owner." Normally, I would introduce myself, but something told me to hold back.

"I was under the impression Mimi Michaels was the store owner," the younger man said and they all nodded.

"She sold it to me a couple of years ago." I slipped my hand into my skirt pocket, hoping to find my phone, but I remembered I left it near the cash register. Turning, I crossed the room, not caring if I appeared rude, and paused at the counter. Very few people made me nervous, but these four definitely brought in the hostility of someone I had wronged. But I had never seen them before.

Milo jumped up on the counter, and without thinking, my hand slid down his back. Just the connection calmed me. He looked up, and in a soft gravelly kitty growl, he said, "Who are they and what are they doing here?"

The brunette looked our way, her eyes fixed on Milo.

I didn't answer him. Was it a coincidence she looked over at the same time he asked his question? Could they be witches from another town and that's how they knew my aunt Mimi?

Milo bobbed his head under my hand as if trying to get some attention. "She can't understand me, but she knows you can."

I could feel my protection necklace that my aunt had given me grow warm against my skin. I turned my back to her and dropped my voice to a whisper. "Who are they?" I glanced over my shoulder and noticed the woman with auburn hair stalking over to me.

"I'm Iris Herman." She pointed to the other woman. "Standing in the historical section behind me is Celeste Jaden. The younger man with her is Clay Proctor and last, but never least, is Luca Rand."

She casually looked over the counter and saw my family's book of magic, *Practical Beginnings*, and her face morphed into a satisfied smile. "Luca. I found it."

Milo jumped on top of it, effectively covering the book with his lanky body.

"I'm sorry that book isn't for sale; it's my family's history."

Luca rushed over and extended his arms, exposing a small moon tattoo. He started to pick up a hissing Milo, who raked his claws down Luca's arms.

His eyes narrowed. "I need to see that book."

Picturing the book in my mind, I said under my breath, "I wrap this book in protection, as I wish so it shall be."

Milo turned slightly and gave me a slow wink. He knew my spell work was getting stronger and better with each passing day. I didn't need a long incantation to make a spell work if the intention was made with strength of spirit.

Luca's eyes widened, and now his attention was focused on me. "Are you related to Mimi?"

The door opened, and Nikki was standing in the doorway. She looked at the people in my shop and then at me. "Morning. Sorry I'm a little late." She closed the door with a flick of her wrist, but it wasn't the non-magical way; she was in witch mode. Her tone was sharp as she said, "What's going on here?"

"Two witches. How interesting." Luca's gaze bored into Nikki, but she didn't flinch.

"We're the Magicians. I'm sure you've heard of our show. We're holding a single performance at the Lights Out movie theatre in town tomorrow night. You should come as our guests." He handed me two tickets that seemed to appear from thin air. When I didn't accept them, he placed the tickets on the counter very close to where my book and Milo were.

This time the low and ominous growl that came from

Milo sounded more like a wild cat ten times his size, and I had never heard that from him before.

Luca withdrew his hand and gave me a smug smile as if to tell me I had won this round but not the war. In my gut, somehow, I knew more skirmishes were to come in regard to my book of magic.

"Clay. Celeste," he called over his shoulder, then inclined his head to give me a sinister smile. "Until next time, Ms. Michaels."

The other two magicians joined Iris and Luca at the counter as Nikki opened the door the way she had closed it, with a flick of her wrist. They filed out the door in a single line, and Luca was the last to leave.

"Nice parlor trick."

Nikki took one step closer to him. Her voice was colder than the wind coming off the ocean as she said, "Tricks are for wannabes."

He lifted a shoulder in a casual shrug. "I look forward to seeing you again."

Without another word, he crossed the threshold. The door slammed behind him, and the lock clicked into place. I could hear Luca chuckle as if Nikki's actions were amusing.

Rushing across the room, she was beside me, wrapping her arms around me in a tight hug. "What was that all about?"

"I'm not sure. But let's not talk about the people who left. I want to hear most of the tidbits of your honeymoon."

Her laughter filled the room, and relief washed over me as the oppressive air in the shop dissipated. She dropped her arm to her side and held up a bakery box. "I haven't fired up the oven yet, so I swung by the Sweet Spot. William had a box of cinnamon pecan buns ready and waiting for me. It was like he knew I'd be by for something sinfully delicious."

"And the coffee should be ready." Milo was still sitting on my book, and I dropped a kiss on his head. "You deserve a special treat."

He stood and stretched his back into an arch. "Smoked salmon?"

Now I laughed. "Not today, and besides, you just had some." I scratched under his chin.

He tipped his chin up so I could scratch a new spot and muttered, "That was over two weeks ago." He hopped down and padded over to the wingback chairs, which was my favorite place to enjoy a hot beverage and a pastry.

Nikki took the bakery box and set it on the small table between the chairs that had a view of the street. The idea that I could watch people in town comforted me since I didn't want the group of magicians to make a repeat visit. But once Nikki took off, I'd give Mimi a call and find out what the scoop was with these people and why they would want my book. A while back, Nikki had tried to help me with a spell, and when she looked at the pages, they were blank. From what my aunt said, only a member of the Michaels family could actually read the book.

I poured coffee into a carafe, then added a sugar bowl and creamer pitcher along with two plates, cups, forks, and napkins. The idea of calling Gage and letting him know what had happened flitted through my mind, but there really wasn't anything to tell other than rude customers wanted to purchase a book that wasn't for sale and then gave us tickets to their performance. Giving them the benefit of the doubt, I thought maybe they had been tired from their trip and that's why the sour moods.

Picking up the tray, I hesitated. I had promised Milo a treat, and he was sitting in my chair, patiently waiting.

I filled a small ball with catnip and rolled it across the floor. "Here you go."

He batted it back to me, and if a cat could cock a brow, he would have. "Tuna, please?"

I knew that snark in his tone, and it was easier to comply than not. Besides, he had protected the book from Luca, so a can of tuna was the very least I could do. Making quick work of opening the can, I filled his bowl and put it on the chair for him. "Milo, thank you for trying to help."

"My dear witch, it's part of my responsibilities as your familiar. And I must say your protection spell has come a long way over the last few months. I could actually feel the surge the moment you cast it. Very powerful indeed."

"Sadly, that is what gave Luca the confirmation I'm a witch. I would have preferred to keep that on the down-low. Non-magicals typically can't handle it."

"Detective Cutie doesn't have an ounce of magic in his veins, despite his mother being a very powerful witch."

I wanted to chuckle at his reference to Gage. "He takes after his father, Burke. But Gage might have some magic in him."

"Glinda's magic would have shown up by now if he had inherited any." He began to eat his tuna. "You know that's the risk you run if you marry him and have kids. They could turn out to take after their father."

I set the tray down on the table and scooped Milo up from the chair, hugging him. "Would that be so bad? Heck, I didn't know I was a witch until a few months ago. It wasn't so bad not having magic."

Milo wriggled out of my arms and dropped down to the floor. "Never say that again! If you had been open to your powers, you'd be a much better witch today." He turned his back to me and waited for me to move his plate of tuna to the floor. When he continued scarfing down the fish, I could have sworn he grumbled, "Not that I didn't try."

I stepped over Milo and joined Nikki who was patiently waiting for me. "Some things haven't changed since you've been honeymooning. Milo and I are still bickering, and I may have overreacted to the situation with Luca Rand and company."

Nikki took the carafe and poured us each a mug of coffee. "That's not how I see it. That guy was not being friendly. He wanted something that you had, and if I hadn't walked in, he might have found a way to get your book. He could be a witch since he made that crack about parlor tricks."

I sniffed. "I protected it and Milo."

She gave me a side-eye. "There was extremely toxic energy when I walked in, and as soon as we're done inhaling our pecan rolls, we're going to smudge the store." Looking around, she said, "You know what, we're not waiting. Come on."

She leaped up and rushed into the back room where I stored various herbs and a few other items like candles for when I had been practicing how to light one. Nikki was on a mission, and I wasn't about to suggest that it could wait.

When she returned, she had an already smoking smudge stick, and she began walking up and down the aisles. I opened the front and back doors and with my arms wide, I tipped back my head and closed my eyes. I could picture myself sweeping out the doors the bad vibes that lingered almost unfelt, but Nikki was right. This was the best thing to do under the circumstances. A short time later we had both finished and I closed the doors by standing in the middle of the room, looking first to the front and then to the back door, willing them to close and lock.

Nikki clapped her hands. "Impressive. When did you learn that?"

"I'm not sure where it came from. I just felt that I could, and it worked." My lips twisted up one side, and I gave her a side-eye look. "Did you just do that for me?"

She held up both hands. "Most definitely not. I never mess with another witch's spell. It's rude."

Now that the shop felt like home again, I gestured to the chair. "Now, let's get down to the most important question. How was the honeymoon?"

"It was great, but you need to fill me in on how you discovered who killed John Bailey and why? And don't leave out the juicy details of how you figured it out before your fiancé."

I smiled when she mentioned Gage, my favorite police detective and the love of my life. "It was all about the treasure and an old family journal." I shook my head from side to side. "Another tragedy, and hopefully our last. The only good things that came out of it was you had a beautiful wedding and we got my aunt's cutlery back."

"I was worried it would never be found after Mimi was gracious enough to allow Steve and me to use it on our wedding day. But why was it taken?"

"Your wedding proved to be the perfect distraction to cover up the real crime."

Nikki handed me a plate with a luscious-looking pecan bun. "Until you put your puzzle skills to work and discovered who had done what."

I took the plate and smiled. "I can say I hope we never have another murder wave in Pembroke Cove again. Five people dying in the span of a few months is just so not good for tourism." I cut the bun with my fork and popped the piece in my mouth, letting the flavors dance across my tongue. "Now the next puzzle that needs to be solved is, how does William knock this recipe out of the oven every single time?"

Chapter 2
Lily

After Nikki left the store, I gave Aunt Mimi a call, but I had to leave a message, so I asked her to stop in later today. Telling her about Luca Rand wasn't critical, but I wanted to ask her advice before the end of the day. Gage and I had plans for dinner, and for once, we weren't having to discuss anything unpleasant, like murder.

A short while later, I had just finished restocking a display when I saw my aunt strolling through the town square. She was carrying a cardboard to-go tray, and that meant time for a break. She was dressed in flowing dark-purple pants and a long cable-knit sweater. A breeze tugged at the ends of a geometric-patterned scarf. Opening the door, I knew my face wore a wide and welcome smile.

"Lily. I got your message and thought a bit of refreshment was just the ticket." She handed me the drink tray and waltzed into the bookstore almost like she still owned it. Not that I minded since she often helped out when I was following a clue or two.

Before securing the door from the blustery wind, I

looked up and down the street. When I didn't see those rude people, I exhaled. For now, they weren't coming back to make another attempt to get my book. Once I closed the door, I walked over to the chairs where Mimi was waiting for me. She waved her finger in a circle around my face.

"It's easy to see you have something weighing heavy on your mind. Tell me what it is, and I can help."

I handed her a cup and inhaled the lingering scent of herbal tea. "You stopped at the Copper Kettle." They were the only shop in town that carried this specific blend of my mother's teas.

Nodding, she said, "I did. When I got your message, I thought this blend would be perfect for whatever was troubling you."

I folded back the lid and carefully took a sip, stalling for the right way to tell her about what had happened earlier. I glanced her way.

With a supportive smile and tilt of her head, she said, "Take your time. I have the rest of the day and night too."

The cup warmed my chilled hands. "Nikki's back, and they had a wonderful time on their honeymoon." I looked over at Milo who was sound asleep on the window seat and remembered how he was right by my side earlier today. He did his best by clawing Luca which slowed the man down when he tried to grab my book.

"A group of people came into the shop earlier. I got the impression they know you."

Aunt Mimi looked me square in the eye. "I ran the shop for many years, and I know a great many people. Do they have names?"

I took a deep ragged breath and exhaled my nerves. Why was I so nervous? Because that feeling in the pit of my gut still lingered even after they left. "Luca Rand and—"

Mimi frowned. "Let me guess, Clay, Iris, and Celeste were with him. I've heard about them but never had the pleasure of actually meeting them."

The somber tone in her voice confirmed my suspicion; they were bad news. "Yes, they said they were in town putting on a show at the theatre, and Luca even gave me and Nikki tickets."

"And what else happened that you're not telling me?" She hadn't moved a muscle, but her left eye twitched.

"Iris assumed Milo was talking to me, and she hurried over to the register. My book, *Practical Beginnings*, was on the counter. They tried to take it from me." Her eyes became as round as saucers, and she wasn't blinking either. All this did was increase my fear that something bad could have happened. "Don't worry. Milo sat on it, and I added a protection spell. At that same moment, Nikki burst through the door looking like a warrior witch."

"With good reason. That little band of people travel around. Now they're going by the moniker *magicians*, but what they are—well, Luca anyway—is a sorcerer."

My brow furrowed. "What is the difference between us and them? We're born magical." I needed to remember to ask Nikki if this was who she had alluded to when she said in the spring other magical beings could show up in town.

Aunt Mimi set her tea aside and clasped her hands in her lap. "Witches are born; sorcerers study and learn how to manipulate props and other items to perform their magic. Much like the magicians you see on television. That's why they're calling themselves the Magicians. At one time they called themselves mage, but it's all the same thing, just different letters in the alphabet."

"Then why do they want my book? Even if they opened it, the pages would appear blank."

She arched a brow. "How did you discover that?"

"Nikki and I were comparing spells, and I gave her my book to look at but the pages were blank." I sipped my tea, and it was having the desired effect—well, that and the conversation with my aunt. I was beginning to regain my equilibrium.

A gleam came into Mimi's eyes. "I'm glad you're discovering the power of the book. But Luca wouldn't know that. What he thinks he knows is the book is powerful, which it is, in the right hands. However, it holds zero value to anyone other than direct descendants of the first Michaels witch."

"Can you read the book even though it's now in my possession?"

Nodding, she said, "I could, but over the years, I've developed my own spell book, also known as a grimoire, and this is more of an academic manual. In fact, you should start to create your own spell book, and I can show you how to enchant it for added protection."

"So, Luca thinks if he possesses the book, he'll have our magic? That makes absolutely no sense in the magical world, does it?"

"You have to remember, Lily, he has some powers, and they might be strong, but he wasn't born a witch. Therefore, he'll never achieve what his ultimate goals are."

I had been sipping my tea while we chatted and suddenly realized the cup was empty. It had bolstered me up just when I needed it the most today. In the moment, I was full of protecting the book and Milo. Now as I'd begun to think about it, I was rattled, and that wasn't something that happened often or easily. "Have you tangled with him before? Is that how he knew you?"

She gave a small, sad smile. "Once, when I was a young woman, Luca and I dated. Even then, he wanted to get his hands on the book, but as soon as I figured out what his real motive was for dating me, I ended it. It's sad that his focus was never altered."

"With any luck, he won't come back to the store."

Patting my hand, she said, "I'm sure they'll do their show and retreat. It is what he always does. Think of it this way, you got to practice casting a spell without much warning." Her eyes twinkled. "Did Milo give you any feedback?"

I sat up straighter in my chair. "Actually, he said my spells have gotten quite powerful. Well, not in those words, but he did say he felt the surge of energy."

Mimi gathered up her handbag and handed me her empty cup. "If you'd like, I can stay until you close up for the day."

We both stood, and I gave her an all-encompassing hug. "Don't be silly. I'm closing up soon, and I have Milo with me, my familiar and bodyguard. I forgot to mention he clawed the bejeebies out of Luca when he tried to take the book."

Laughing, she said, "I'll bet the look on Luca's face was priceless. You need to get cameras just in case there is another incident where footage would be fun to replay."

I looped my arm through hers and steered her to the front door. "I won't be installing cameras. That would give me an icky feeling to know my every move was recorded, and in this era, we don't need footage of me dancing around the shop to get on the internet or something. Either business would dry up and I'd be considered an oddity or people would come in droves, not to shop but just to see what I might do." I chuckled. "Now that might be something Luca would want. It would give him a chance to swoop in and steal the book while I was boogying down."

Aunt Mimi's laughter was the final bit of salve I needed

to feel like I could go back and conquer the world again. "Thanks for coming over."

"I'm always here for you, Lily, and don't forget it." She looked around the room. "You did a very good job with the cleanse."

"Nikki and I did it together."

Placing her hand under my chin and tilting it up so she could look into my eyes, she said, "You are stronger together, but remember the power of three. If you must, ask another witch for help. We're a community ready to support one another."

Holding up my pointer finger, I said, "That reminds me, do we have coven meetings or just always doing our own thing and happen to find out about each other as time drifts by?"

Patting my cheek, she said, "I'll make sure you and Dax are invited to the next coven meeting, and for the record, they're held quarterly." With a flutter of her fingertips, she eased out the door, humming a little tune that seemed vaguely familiar.

I had just enough time to clean up the store and figure out what I was going to wear for my date tonight. But first, Milo needed to be awake to help. If nothing else, he could watch for customers.

"Wake up, sleepyhead. Time to earn your salmon."

I tickled his ears, and he slowly opened one eye and glared at me. "Did you say salmon or smoked salmon? And are you using bribery to get me to do something?"

I scooped him up and laughed. "It depends. I need you to watch the store so I can tidy up the back before we head home."

He yawned, and I could see a row of very sharp teeth

and was glad he hadn't bitten Luca since they might leave a scar.

"That can be arranged." He gave me a quick glance. "Do you have a date tonight with the detective or someone else?"

I held up my left hand and wriggled my fingers so my diamond sparkled in the weak sunlight. "Did you forget we're engaged?"

"Right. A familiar can still hope you'd decide to marry a witch, but if you have to marry a non-magical, there are worse options."

I plopped him on the counter and patted his head. "Thanks for the support."

Milo swished his tail. "Anytime." He stretched out across the top and said, "Let me know when it's time to leave. I don't want to walk home today."

Giving him an exaggerated bow, I said, "At your service."

He grumbled, "Now we're talking."

After back and forth texts about what Gage and I should do for dinner, we agreed a nice quiet meal at my place was perfect. Now with our plates empty, Milo stretched across the back of the sofa, and Brutus, Gage's Great Dane rescue, in front of us, we sat with our fingers entwined as the fire flickered in the pellet stove. It was just cool enough outside for the fire to make everything cozy.

"I had some excitement today at the store." I told him everything that happened with Luca and even about Nikki coming into the shop like a superhero, and he chuckled.

"I can picture her now. Nobody messes with her bestie.

But what's the story with these people? Do you think they'll be back to harass you?"

I squeezed his hand. "Don't go getting all cop on me. I'm fine, and besides, I talked to Aunt Mimi about them today. She is sure they'll do their show and move on."

"How can she be so confident?" He lifted our joined hands to his lips and kissed the back of my hand. "He's a stranger."

My heart thumped a little quicker in my chest at the sweet gesture. "Yes and no. It seems a very long time ago, they briefly dated."

"That's a twist I didn't see coming."

I laughed. "I never thought of her as dating anyone but Nate, and now that they're married, I could never picture her with anyone else."

He smiled and shifted on the sofa to put his arm around me. "Like us?" He tenderly kissed my mouth.

I sighed. "Yes, like us."

Cupping my cheek, he asked, "Are you ready to set a date for our wedding?"

I hadn't expected that question, but some people got baby fever after a friend had one, and I'm guessing since our best friends just got married a couple of weeks ago, he was feeling the tug. "I love you very much, but we've only been engaged a few months."

"Um, six months but who's counting." He brushed a stray lock of my short hair from my eyes.

I dropped my head. "Let's make a deal. We will set a date on our anniversary."

"Which one? Our friendship, our romance, or our engagement?" His eyes twinkled.

"Exactly." I pecked his lips. "One of these days I'll surprise you."

"Oh, my sweet Lily, you surprise me every day now, and I'm sure it will continue for the rest of our lives."

Milo began to gag which turned into trying to cough up a hairball. From his spot on the back of the couch, he grumbled, "Put Detective Cutie out of his misery, and set a date, will you? The sooner I know when they'll be moving in, the better."

Gage tipped his head and gave me a quizzical look. "What's Milo saying?"

I grinned. "He's on your side and wants us to set a date. He just brought up a good question, though. Where are we going to live after we're married? Here or at your house?"

He looked around the cozy living room. "I'm happy as long as you're next to me."

Milo began to cough again. "Puh-leeze. But in that case, it's settled. We're not moving. They are."

"And Milo's latest comment?"

Glancing at Brutus and then Milo, I said, "Looks like we'll be living here, but we might need to add on since we have two pets and who knows, maybe someday..."

Gage gave me a slow kiss. "Then at least one thing is settled. We can start making plans for a few minor house changes."

I looked at Milo, and he gave me a slow kitty wink. "Well done, my dear witch."

Chapter 3
Gage

The following morning, after my date with Lily, I had just walked into the police station when my cell rang. I checked caller ID and smiled. "Hello there, you couldn't wait to talk to me?"

"Gage, come quick. I'm at the bookshop, and there's been an accident. A shelf has toppled over, and a man is trapped underneath it."

"I'll call for the ambulance."

I heard her suck in a ragged breath. "Call a hearse." Her voice was devoid of emotion. "He's dead."

"Who's dead?"

"I'm not sure, but there's a hand sticking out, and he doesn't have a pulse. And I can't see his face, but based on what I can see, it is definitely a man."

"I'll be there as fast as I can. And don't touch anything in the shop." I was already striding in the direction of the exit when Dax Peters was on his way in. He was a recent addition to the force and had quickly become my trusted friend.

"Where are you headed in such a rush?" He fell in step

next to me as I began to run across Doenut Drive and through the town park.

"Lily's got a dead body under a bookcase in the shop."

Thankfully, he didn't ask any other questions as we made it to the shop in less than five minutes. He understood there was no time to waste with Lily potentially in danger. She had a way of finding trouble, especially when she wasn't looking for it.

Her head snapped in my direction, cheeks flushed, eyes wide. "I just came in through the back door and found this." She gestured to a five-foot-wide section of a bookcase that had crashed to the floor. Books were everywhere, and just as Lily had said, all that was visible was a hand.

My first instinct was to fold Lily in my arms, but I had a job to do. "Dax, give Peabody and Mac a call, and let them know what we're facing."

"You got it, Gage." He moved to the front of the store, leaving me with Lily.

"Any idea how he got in the store? Or how the shelves toppled over?"

She slowly shook her head and chewed on the corner of her lip. The stress of the situation was showing. "Both doors were locked, and I know I didn't leave someone in the store overnight. Also, those shelves are secured with heavy-duty bolts."

That idea had never crossed my mind. "I know you're very careful, but he had to have gotten in here some way."

She flicked a frown in my direction. "Don't you think I've already asked myself that a bunch of times since the moment I saw him and then called you?"

I slung an arm around her shoulders and pulled her to my side. I felt her straighten, and then she knelt down close to the hand but not touching it. She looked up at me. "I think this is Luca Rand, the man who was in my shop yesterday."

"What makes you say that?"

"Look at the small half-moon tattoo on the visible part of his wrist." She gestured to the radial portion of the hand. "I saw that yesterday when Milo scratched Luca, and I'll bet when we can see his entire arm, we'll see evidence of Milo's attack. But what would he have been doing in the shop? Looking for my book?"

The shock of finding a dead man in her shop had disappeared, and her inquisitive mind kicked in. "It's a possibility, but maybe something else caught his interest when he was poking around."

Lily stood up and crossed her arms over her body. "Now, what might have been on that shelf that would have interested him?"

I could hear the police siren of the squad car growing closer and walked outside to talk with my officers. Dax was on the sidewalk and said, "Lily sure does have a knack for getting involved with murder."

My blood chilled. I didn't like how that sounded. "She's not involved. It was an unfortunate accident."

He gave me a side-eye. "Six bodies and she's been on the scene for all of them."

"An unfortunate coincidence. Nothing more." That statement didn't annoy me as much as it struck a chord in my gut. It was as if she was a murder magnet, but I knew there was no such thing.

Mac got out from the driver's side, and Peabody was striding to the trunk where she stored the forensic kit.

Mac came around carrying one case. He nodded in my direction. "Detective, is Lily alright?"

"She was a little shaken, but in true Lily fashion, she bounced back already."

Mac gave me a guarded smile. "I'm sure."

Peabody walked up. Her eyes were serious. "Any idea who the victim is?"

With a single nod, I said, "Lily thinks it's a man who was in her shop yesterday. He tried to take her family history book."

She arched a brow and cocked her head to the side. "Why would he want something personal to her family?"

Peabody and Mac were both non-magical people and unaware that witches were living among us, and I intended to keep it that way. "It's a mystery."

The officers entered the shop, and Lily was slipping her cell phone back in her pocket. Without having seen what she had been up to, I knew she had been taking pictures on her phone, and the clue board she kept stored in her pantry closet would be set up in her kitchen by the end of the day. I didn't need for Lily to be investigating this crime. In each of the last five instances, she had barely escaped with her life.

"Sharon." Lily gave her a small smile. She was the only person in town who called Peabody by her given name. "We need to stop meeting like this."

Peabody touched her arm. "At least you don't need to be told not to touch anything at the scene of the crime."

Lily flashed me a sarcastic look, knowing that I always said that to her, but it was a force of habit and not because I ever thought she'd contaminate a scene. I shrugged and mouthed, *I'm sorry.*

Mac had the camera in hand and was walking around the bookcase, taking plenty of pictures, both close-up and farther away. "Are you ready to lift this off?"

Lily wiped her hands on her dark-washed jeans. "I'll help."

Despite that, this was Lily, I needed to follow procedure by the book. "I need you to wait over at the counter, and we'll take care of the rest."

"Really?"

Her voice was frosty, but I couldn't risk any clue being overlooked because I was distracted by my fiancée. "Lily, please."

She threw up her hands and stamped her feet across the bookstore, picking up Milo from a chair on the way, then set him on the counter. The fact he was totally unconcerned with all that was going on wasn't surprising since this would give him and Lily time to chat.

Milo's eyes locked on our every move just like his witch's did too. "Peabody, document each step as we lift this off our victim."

"That only leaves you with three people," Lily called out from her vantage point. "My offer stands. I can take pictures too."

She was relentless when we both knew all she wanted was a good look and maybe even the first look at the victim.

"Lily." I made sure my voice was firm and held a slight warning tone.

She threw up her hands. "Can't blame a girl for trying."

I pointed to what was the top of the case. "Dax, since you're taller than Mac, will you take that spot and Mac, grab the other end. On three, we'll lift it up and back."

"Right," Mac said and Dax moved into position.

I did a quick countdown, and with all the books on the floor, it was fairly easy to lift it up and off. Peabody was snapping pictures, and we muscled the bookcase close to the one behind him. "Lily, are any of these freestanding without being secured?"

"No, each one is anchored to the wall. We'd never take a chance of something like this toppling over."

I waved her over to my side. "Is that Luca Rand?"

She didn't need to take a long look. "It is." Pointing to his other hand, she said, "What's he holding on to?"

Peabody handed Mac the camera, and she tossed me a pair of gloves and an evidence bag. "Detective."

I grabbed them in midair. "Thanks." I waited for Mac to give me the all clear before I pushed aside a few books so I could get a closer look at what the victim was clutching.

I eased the crumpled paper out and pressed it flat and held up a key. It was an ad from the local newspaper for the Cozy Nook Bookshop. It had the days and hours not only listed but circled in red marker. I slipped the paper into the evidence bag and passed it to Dax. He took a look, glanced at me, and then passed it to Peabody who did the same. Next, I added the key. I was going to check to see if it fit the lock on the doors to the store, but without doing that, I had a sinking feeling it would.

Luca Rand knew exactly when Lily would be closed, so I was going to make a quick guess that his sneaking in had to do with trying to find her book of magic. But that theory only worked if he was magical too.

I could feel Lily watching me. When I looked up, I said, "Do you know anything about him or his friends?"

"Nothing more than what I told you last night. He said they were in town for a performance for just one night."

"He was with three other people. Did they happen to say where they're staying?"

She paused. "No, I don't think that came up. But there's

only two choices close to town. Pembroke Cove B & B or the motel out on Route One."

Donnie White had hired a new manager for Pembroke Cove after a man had been killed three weeks ago over a pirate treasure. So, it was a possibility. "Peabody, when we're done here, you and Mac stop at the B & B, and if they're not staying there, try the motel. We need to track down his companions and tell them the news."

"Do you want to be the one to inform them of the victim's recent circumstances?"

I wanted to chuckle at how Peabody phrased it but didn't. "Escort them to the station. That way we can have an informal conversation at the same time."

Nodding, she said, "I'll text you when we've located them."

As Mac was finishing up taking pictures, the EMTs showed up to take the body to the hospital so an autopsy could be performed. They made quick work of loading the ambulance and leaving.

I looked at the books that were on the floor around him. Some were focused on local history, and the balance were random titles. On the other side of the bookcase were at least fifteen Agatha Christie books that were placed on the floor. I didn't want to disturb anything else when I noticed a pendant half-hidden under a book. It looked vaguely familiar. "Dax, toss me another evidence bag."

Withdrawing a pen from my jacket pocket and using the tip, I snagged the necklace. The pendant dangled in the morning sun for a fraction of a moment before I slipped it into the bag. I turned the bag over in my hand, and I looked at Lily.

Her eyes widened. "Is that my necklace?"

I stepped closer to her and held it up. "You recognize this? It's yours?"

Her hand flew to her chest and patted the front of her blouse. Her face blank with shock, she asked, "How did that get over there?"

"When was the last time you remember wearing it?" This was more of a standard question, not that I thought Lily did anything wrong even if it was close to where we had just discovered a body. This was her shop, and she could have dropped it at any time.

"Yesterday. It got warm when Luca was trying to take the book. That happens from time to time during certain situations."

She didn't elaborate on what specifically those situations were, and with Peabody and Mac around, I didn't press it. There would be time for more questions later.

Lily extended her hand. "Can I have it back? It's very special to me." She dropped her gaze. "Aunt Mimi gave it to me around the time she was accused of killing Flora."

I remembered when our librarian died. That was when Lily discovered she was a witch. My mom wore a similar necklace, and there were several other people in town who each also wore one that resembled this design. It made sense that it had something do to with the witches of Pembroke Cove.

"It's part of a crime scene, so I can't give it back just yet, but maybe in a few days. Hopefully."

I handed the bag to Dax who took it and shot a glance at Lily. He said, "I'm sure there's a logical explanation for how it got there."

"Is the clasp broken?" I pointed at the bag since the thought had just occurred to me.

He took a closer look. "Not that I can tell."

"Gage, this necklace doesn't have a normal type of clasp. It's special." She looked to see if Peabody and Mac were paying any attention or interested in the conversation. "I always slip it on and off, so it shouldn't be weak."

But the unspoken truth, it was magical, and the only way it could have been taken from her was by other means. I shuddered to think of her alone with these people, four against one. Well, except when Nikki showed up. Together their friendship and magic were powerful. They would be formidable when they joined forces. At least that was what I'd witnessed years ago when Mimi and my mother worked together on an incident involving an angry mermaid.

Peabody said, "Lily, do you have any idea if you were wearing your necklace when you left for the day last night?"

My heart sank. "You had it on during dinner."

Her mouth dropped open and she whispered, "I did."

Chapter 4
Lily

I slumped into a wingback chair as Sharon and Mac finished taking pictures and collecting evidence. Dax was in the back room making me a cup of tea while Gage sat next to me, holding my hand. Milo, my sweet baby, jumped into my lap, turned three times, then curled up into a snuggly ball. "Don't worry, Lily," he grumbled, "it's going to be all right." His reassurance was comforting, but if this was another crime scene, with such few clues, I would be the primary suspect. I looked Gage directly in the eyes and took his hand. "I promise you I had nothing to do with this."

He gave me a reassuring smile. "Don't you think I know that? You didn't even have to say the words."

"Are you going to check the key to see if it fits the locks?" The tension in the air was palpable as I asked the question. "And we both know it will, so why even bother."

"It's a formality, and there is a chance that it won't." Gage placed his hand on my cheek and turned my face to his. "Come on, you need to stop going down that path. I know you had nothing to do with this man's death even if he was found here."

My heart was heavy in my chest. "What was on the paper?" It had looked like a newspaper from a distance, but I wasn't sure what it could have been, and the specifics were the only thing that would keep my name clear.

"I shouldn't be telling you, but it was an advertisement for your shop with the hours listed."

Nodding my head, I sat in silence, ideas spinning. This must tie back to the Michaels' book of *Practical Beginnings*. Luca knew about it from when he dated my aunt, but why was it so important to him? I stood up. It was time for action, and sitting around here wasn't going to change the fact that he died in my store. Was it murder? It had to be since the bookshelf should have been firmly attached to the wall.

"We have to talk to his companions, and I'll call Aunt Mimi. She and Luca were friendly many years ago, although she didn't have a lot to say about him when we talked yesterday."

Sharon and Mac gathered up the evidence kits, and she said, "Detective, we're headed back to the station, and on the way, we'll stop at the B & B."

"Good. I have a hunch the magicians are staying at the motel. When you find them, make sure they understand they need to come to the station."

"Certainly." Sharon placed a hand on my shoulder and gave it a light squeeze. "Hang in there, Lily."

I didn't say anything as they left the store.

Dax returned with a mug, and he set it on the table in front of me. Gage nodded to him. "Can you follow up with Peabody, and as soon as the other magicians are on their way to the station, let me know."

I crossed to the shop door and made sure the CLOSED sign was in place. "I'm going with you, and before you say no, I can be in the room that has the one-way mirror when you talk to them."

The hangdog look in his eyes said more than his words would. Whether either of us liked it or not, I was the prime suspect in this death, and until it was ruled accidental, there was no way I could be within one hundred feet of the investigation. But all that meant was I needed to get home and set up my clue board. There was much more to this than met the eye other than Luca Rand being in my store and searching for the unknown.

"I know that look, Lily." He reached out and touched my cheek. "You have to stay out of the investigation until I know for sure what happened."

Tipping up my chin, I countered, "Does that mean you'll share what you learn from the coroner?"

"Why can't you let this go and let me do my job?"

I stamped my foot, the sound muffled by the area rug. "I found a man dead in my bookstore. Stars only know how many times I'm going to need to smudge the building before I can get rid of the bad energy. Nikki and I had to do that yesterday when he left the building with Clay, Iris, and Celeste."

Gage placed his hands on my shoulders. Under normal circumstances, I would take comfort in his dreamy hazel eyes. The way his brown hair fell over his forehead made me want to reach up and smooth it back. But I had heard the firm tone in his voice just moments before.

"You need to trust me. I will take care of everything, and when this is all over, I'll get every witch I know to come down and cleanse the shop just to make sure there are no remnants of bad energy. Including Glinda."

His mom was at the top of my favorite witches in town list but that wasn't enough to provide me with comfort.

However, arguing with Gage about sharing the intel wasn't going to do me a bit of good. It was best to acquiesce and get home, so that I could start a parallel investigation.

His cell dinged with an incoming message. "I need to see who that is."

I stepped back, giving him the privacy he needed, and jammed my hands in my pants pockets. Yellow crime scene tape was around the perimeter of books outlining the space where Luca had lain. I shivered just thinking about the books and wooden bookcase falling on him. Had he died instantly or was it a slow and painful passing?

"Lily, I have to go." Gage moved closer to the door. "But I need to ask you to lock up and leave with me and don't come back alone."

My shoulders sagged. "You've got to be kidding?"

"Bubbles, it's for your protection."

Ah, and when he started calling me by my old nickname, I knew he was serious. It would be best for both of us if we worked together instead of me butting up against him at every turn.

"I need to turn off the coffee pot, lock the back door, and get my bag. You can even search it if you want."

"Actually, I'm going to ask Dax to check it out. Just to keep everything in the proper chain of command."

I stuck out my wrists as my anger covered my hurt. "Do you want to arrest me now too?" I knew I was overreacting, but I didn't care. All this follow procedure nonsense, just being cautious, proper chain of command, it broke my heart. This was my fiancé talking to me like I was a suspect in this crime.

He shook his head and looked absolutely crestfallen. "I need to go, so Dax will stay." Heading for the door, he paused midstep and said, "Don't be mad at me, be mad at the situation." He stepped outside. With one final look, he strode in the direction of the police station.

As I watched him go, I was at a complete loss for words. It seemed like we were at war with each other but not in the same battle.

Dax closed the door, and I gave him a once-over. Anxious for a distraction, I said, "What happened to the new clothes we bought a couple of weeks ago?"

He looked at his black jeans, jacket, and white button-down shirt. "This is like wearing an old shoe. It's comfortable and just me."

I popped out my right hip and rested my hand on it. "Tired of blending in?"

He grinned. "Why would I want to do that when one of my best friends doesn't."

Milo stalked across the room, and I realized he had been strangely silent with all the commotion. He looked at Dax and then at me and gave me a lazy wink. "Dax, you're going to have to choose sides between Lily and Gage. Because she's about to jump into this investigation with both feet, and if you want to hang around, you can't be running down the street to tell Detective Cutie everything that goes on."

He laughed which broke the tension that had hung heavy in the air since the moment I saw Luca's hand sticking out from under the bookcase.

"Just a question before I take sides."

I arched a brow and glanced at Milo who said, "He's your friend, only my acquaintance."

Dax clutched the center of his black shirt in mock horror. "You wound me, Milo."

He lifted a paw and began to wash his face. "The only reason I'm talking to you at all is because you saved Lily during the second haunted Halloween event."

I suppressed a smile. Milo had a way of getting right to the point. I was pleased that he was always ready to jump to my defense in any way he could. "Here's how it's going down, Detective." Once I had Dax's full attention, I said, "You're going to check my bag as directed by Detective Erikson, and then you're going to check to make sure both doors are locked and I'm going home. If you would like to meet me there, that's fine, or if you would rather stick to the letter of the law, then head back to the police station. We need to know the whereabouts of his three traveling companions."

His eyes widened for a brief moment. "Where's your bag? And I'll just head back and check the rear exit."

Very sweetly, I said, "On your way, can you make sure the coffee pot is off too?" I winked at Milo. Dax was going to be in our corner and now I had a mole. I was beginning to feel more like a real private investigator with each case I worked on.

When Dax came back, I handed him my bag. "It's all secured back there, and the pot is off and unplugged. No sense wasting electricity." He glanced in the bag, giving it a cursory look and said, "Now let's get you on your way since I need to head back to the station."

"And?" I scooped up Milo, and we went out the front entrance. My blue and white Mini Coop was sitting next to the curb.

Dax jiggled the doorknob, satisfied it was locked, but we both knew it wouldn't take much for me to unlock it and stroll back inside; however, this was all for the the benefit of non-magicals, like Sharon and Mac.

"As soon as I know anything, I'll let you know." He gave me a quick brotherly hug. "But you need to lay low. Stay home and think about what Rand might have been looking for at the shop and talk to Mimi again. You said they knew each other. Since events have changed, she might have different ideas."

"Thanks for being on my side." I opened my car door, Milo hopped into the passenger seat, and I put my bag on the floor in the back.

"To be clear, I'm not taking sides, but I know that if you don't have someone to confide in and look to for help without judgment, you'll go off on your own, and I don't want anything to happen to you. So, until we know the truth, we're in this together."

I slowly nodded. "Don't get any ideas about becoming my Watson again. Nikki is back, and if you could have seen her in action yesterday, she is one tough witch."

His forehead crinkled, and his eyes narrowed. "What happened?"

I quickly set the scene for him when Iris and Luca were trying to take the book and how Milo had scratched Luca. I finished my story with, "And then Nikki entered the shop like my personal bodyguard, ready to take on the world and anyone in it."

He threw his head back and laughed, clutching his midsection as he did. Why he thought that was so funny was beyond me.

"I wish I could have seen that. I knew she was tough as nails, but to face down a group of strangers, that had to have been priceless."

"She succeeded in making her point. That along with Luca's arm covered in deep scratches and the blood." I shuddered, remembering the pain Milo inflicted on my behalf. "Suffice it to say, the last twenty-four hours have been too eventful for me to let this go and leave it to Gage and the police to discover what happened."

Dax's smile faded from his face. "I hope to have some answers for you soon, but be careful and keep your doors locked."

"Did you forget I'm a witch?"

He sighed. "You are a talented witch, but you're still learning. I know Gage couldn't feel the bad energy in your shop, but I could. A very strong force was behind what happened in there."

I let his words sink in before asking, "Are you saying that Luca Rand was murdered in my shop?"

"Yes. That is exactly what I'm saying, and the key that was used had a residue of magic on it. You need to be very careful." He glanced in the back seat. "Where is your book of magic?"

"It's at home. Why?"

"Based on what you said, that book is the key for this entire thing, and if I'm not mistaken, someone is planning on setting you up to take the fall. You need to be very careful, and I've got your back."

"I'm going to call Nikki and fill her in. Between the three of us, we'll solve this mystery. I'm going to set up my clue board as soon as I get home." I slid behind the wheel and looked up at Dax. "Are you going to tell Gage most of what you know?"

"Yeah, he'll get the magic stuff being that his mom is a witch, but it's not something he can put in the report. Even though he won't be thrilled to know that I'm supporting you in what we know is going to morph into you investigating. The connection to bad magic will make it easier for him to accept."

He tapped the roof of my car. "Do me a favor and shoot me a text when you get home. Call it being a good brother if you want but"—he rolled his shoulders—"I just have a bad feeling about this one, Lily, and you're dead center of it all."

A chill raced down my spine, and I promised to text when I got home. He closed the door and started walking at a fast clip in the opposite direction. As soon as I started my car, I called Nikki. When she answered, I said, "Can you meet me at my place in ten minutes? I'm in trouble, and I need your help."

Chapter 5
Lily

By the time I walked through the door later that morning, I was ready to roll up my sleeves and track down the truth about what had happened in my store. Before I set up my clue board, I sent Dax a quick text confirming all was well. Milo had settled on a kitchen chair and promptly curled into a ball and fell asleep. I swear my familiar had no sense of impending doom at all.

Once my clue board was in place, I sent the pictures to my laptop so I could print them. I was pretty sure Gage had seen me clicking away but decided to overlook my actions. While I was waiting for the printer to shoot out color copies, I called Aunt Mimi. I was dreading telling her about my necklace since I had no idea how it ended up at the store long before I had arrived.

My phone rang before I could dial. Answering on the first ring, I said, "Hi, Aunt Mimi."

"Lily, I wanted to make sure you were home before I came over so that you can tell me everything. Do you need anything? Tea, cookies, a cozy blanket to crawl under?"

That brought a smile to my face. "Aunt Mimi, you know

the Michaels women are not the type to cower under a blanket when there is trouble brewing."

"I know you can't help it that your favorite auntie was trying to lighten the mood. Rumor has it you've had a bad day."

"Let's put it this way. I hope I have a big enough smudge stick to cleanse the shop once Gage releases it back to me."

"That bad?"

I could hear the empathy in her voice. "The person was Luca Rand, and for the rest of the story, I think you should come over. Nikki is on her way, and we can talk about what I know, things I'm guessing at, and come up with a hypothesis."

"Give me fifteen minutes, maybe twenty, and I'll be there."

After agreeing I'd wait for her, I disconnected and put a kettle of water on the old-fashioned way, by actually filling the kettle from the spigot and placing it on a burner to heat. There was something soothing about going through the motions of making tea.

My hand rested on my chest. I was unnerved by the absence of my necklace, the one my aunt had given me when I learned I was a witch. It would get warm to the touch when danger was around me. Crossing to the chalkboard, I began to write down the events from yesterday.

Magicians come to town, LR, CP, CJ, IH – where are they now?

Iris alerted Luca about my book

Luca tries to take it – Milo claws him

They leave seemingly amiably

Got to store 8-ish- found bookcase on body

My necklace

Key and paper clipping

LR dated Mimi

I didn't have anything more to add at this point. Stepping back, I moved on autopilot, filling an infuser with a blend of green tea, peppermint, and a piece of honeycomb in the bottom of the teapot. This would be the perfect lift for brain power and concentration, besides tasting delish.

Milo opened one eye and yawned. "Lily, I'm curious about something?"

I leaned against the counter and waited for him to continue. I had learned rushing my familiar never got him to the point any faster.

"When Mimi gave you the necklace, it had to have been magically infused for protection, and I know you never take it off. Last night, did you take it off and put it on the bedside table?"

I tipped my head, not because I thought I had taken it off, but I felt like I had dreamed about it, but it was just out of reach. Like a song that you can't quite remember, but it slowly becomes the earworm for half of a memory. "I haven't taken it off since she gave it to me."

Milo arched his back as he stretched. "Interesting, and I went out for a while last night, the monthly meeting for the area familiars, so I wasn't home until very late."

"Really? Why didn't you tell me you were going out?"

"At the time, it wasn't relevant. It was after your detective went home and you were going to bed. When these meetings occur, I'm gone for a couple of hours, and you sleep. It gets me out of the house, and I avoid your snoring for a while."

Folding my arms over my stomach, I said, "The only snoring in this house is from that little snout of yours."

He jumped down and flicked his tail from side to side.

"You can believe that if you like, but one of these nights I'm going to turn on your phone and record you."

He strolled out of the room, getting the last word for now since there was no way I could refute real evidence, and he knew it. Besides, I'd woken myself up from time to time, and the only person in the room had been me. I knew I snored, but I wasn't about to fess up to him.

A tapping on the back door drew my attention. I crossed the room and opened the door. Nikki was balancing a bakery box as well as a pizza. "Lunch and dessert," she said as she came in. Before I could close the door, I heard Aunt Mimi calling to me, so I waited for her to come up the back steps. She was holding a bottle of wine in each hand.

"We can have this before or after tea." She kissed my cheek and seemed to float into the kitchen. "Nikki," she said, "it's so good that you're home. Our Lily is going to need help finding the truth around the current circumstances." She put the wine bottles down and slipped out of her coat, tossing it over the back of a chair.

Rubbing her hands together, she said, "Where do we start?" Aunt Mimi was like a whirlwind in a good way.

"With tea. I've brewed up a green and mint blend for concentration." I handed my aunt three pretty floral cups and carried the pot to the kitchen table that had a clear view of the board. "I'll review my notes."

Aunt Mimi looked at my clue board and gasped. "What's this about your necklace?"

I could feel the heat flush my cheeks a deep shade of red. "I was going to tell you about that." Before I could say any more, Mimi did a slow three-sixty in the room and walked down the hall in the direction of my bedroom. I was glad I had taken the time to tidy everything this morning and put away the clean clothes from the basket. I'd hate for her and Nikki to think I was a slob. But what was she doing?

Aunt Mimi closed her eyes, tipped back her head, and with her arms outstretched, she began to talk under her breath. I couldn't understand what she was saying, and I cast a questioning look to Nikki. Maybe she knew what was going on. But she shrugged her shoulders and we waited in silence.

After several long minutes that seemed to drag on for an eternity, Mimi opened her eyes and dropped her arms. "Someone has been in here and cast a spell. It was during those few moments they took your necklace from you by magic."

I looked at my sock-covered feet. "Thank the stars I didn't lose it from being careless." I lifted my chin. "That proves that someone took it and left it at the bookstore. It had to have been Luca, right?"

Aunt Mimi shook her head. "He's not a witch, so there's no way he could have gotten in here, removed your necklace, and left without waking you. It was clearly a spell. But I don't recognize the energy that remains."

I gave her a quizzical look. "Why do you say that? Does magic leave a marker like perfume?"

She thought for a moment. "That's a good way to describe it."

I looked at Nikki and asked. "Do you?"

"No, to a witch that's not as skilled, they leave a signature. As their craft is refined, it fades."

It was the finality in Nikki's answer that caused my heart to sink a little. My hand went back to where my necklace should have been, and I felt not quite myself. I hadn't realized how much a part of me the pendant had become until it was gone. "Why didn't I notice it was gone as soon as I woke up this morning?"

Nikki looked at Mimi. "An educated guess is it was part of the spell. Until it was discovered in the shop, you weren't meant to realize it."

The first piece of the puzzle clicked into place, but I had no way to prove it yet. "Luca was murdered, and someone is trying to frame me for the crime."

Aunt Mimi's mouth was turned down, her eyes filled with sorrow and concern. She took my hand and held it tight. "That is the logical assumption at this point. However, now that we know someone was in your house in the last twelve hours, there are things we can do in an attempt to discover who it was."

"Do you think the person responsible could be working with a local witch? I know there are many people in town who I don't know if they're magical or not."

"There isn't one witch within a one-hundred-mile radius or maybe the entire northeast who would help anyone cast a spell against a Michaels witch."

I cocked a brow. "Really, Aunt Mimi? I'm not all that special. I'm refining my ability to cast spells without tons of planning and flawlessly execute them. In the beginning it was pure luck, now I want to be intentional in all I do."

When Nikki looked at Mimi's expression, she burst out laughing. "She doesn't know, does she?"

My aunt shook her head. "I wasn't about to overwhelm her as she started to learn her craft, but since I've kind of let the cat out of the bag, I'll need to fill her in." She didn't continue but turned and left the room.

Slack-jawed, I said to Nikki, "What is going on?"

She gestured to my aunt. "Follow her. And don't worry,

I'm right behind you since there is no way I'm going to miss this reveal."

I wasn't sure if I should be nervous or excited at the cloak and wand at hand. With no other choice, in my opinion, I hurried down the hall into the kitchen where my aunt was pouring tea.

"Lily, slip the pizza in the oven to keep it warm." Nikki took a seat next to my aunt who handed her a cup of tea and flashed me a small grin.

I did as Mimi asked. Even though she could have warmed the pizza magically, this would give us both time to gather our thoughts. Well for me, questions that I didn't even know what they might be. For my aunt, the best way to divulge a deep secret, one that my best friend apparently knew. I was going to have to chat with her about all these secrets she had kept from me, and it had all started when she knew I was a witch and never told me.

Once I was sitting down, I took the teacup Mimi offered me and sipped. The honey was the perfect balance to the green and mint tea and I didn't speak until the cup was empty. I wasn't sure where to even begin. Was it even my place to spill the cauldron of whatever Aunt Mimi had alluded to? I was a decent poker player so I could wait.

Nikki looked between the two of us. "Will one of you start talking? The silence is going to kill me."

I tipped my head to the side. "It's really not up to me. I'm not the one keeping a family secret."

My aunt got a gleam in her eye and smiled. "Touché. But I wasn't sure if you even wanted to know the history of our family. Ever since you opened the book, *Practical Beginnings*, you've never asked about anything other than how to do certain spells."

"I didn't know there was more to learn. We're witches. I

would guess we've been around for a while, and since our family goes back generations in Pembroke Cove, it would stand to reason that our special talent has been around as long."

"True, and since you're not really asking me questions, I'll skip the boring beginning and talk about what is relevant here since, if my intuition is correct, time is of the essence."

Now she had piqued my curiosity. I sat up straighter in my chair, slid my now empty teacup away from me, and leaned forward. A gleam came into Mimi's eyes, and she nodded approvingly.

My eyes locked on my aunt's. "Is our ability to do magic the driving force to what happened to Luca?"

"Indirectly. It's the position we hold within the witch community, and as of this moment, since you have no children, you are the last Michaels witch."

"Now isn't the time to bring up the fact that I haven't had kids yet." At least she wasn't like my mom. Now that Gage and I were engaged, she had asked me point-blank if I had talked with him about having a family. We haven't, and I'm a traditionalist—first, the wedding.

Aunt Mimi made a circular motion around my face. "I know where your mind just went, and that's not what I'm referring to."

"You two are killing me," Nikki blurted out. "What your aunt is alluding to is the Michaels witches are like royalty. Your aunt is the queen, and you're the queen-in-waiting."

My mouth dropped open. I was stunned. "What..." I stammered. "We're what?"

Aunt Mimi gave a sheepish shrug. "Someday when I'm gone, you'll be in charge of the"—she made air quotes— "coven."

I slumped in my chair. "Okay, so let me get this straight.

Being me, a late blooming witch, has put me in line to run a coven I basically don't know anything about, and Luca's murder has something to do with it, and someone who practices dark magic broke into my home, somehow removed my necklace off my body, then using a key which they probably stole from me as well, broke into my store, toppled a bookcase filled with books which weighed several hundred pounds on top of a magician who earlier in the day tried to take our book of magic, all to unseat me as the next in line?" I took a deep breath and exhaled after my very long sentence.

Mimi nodded and said, "Yes."

I smacked my head with the palm of my hand. "There is no way Gage can put that down on a murder board as the motive for Luca Rand's death. Sharon and Mac would never believe him or it."

Aunt Mimi gave me a firm look. "Then we need to repackage the truth so he has something to write down because I guarantee you, this is the motive.

And I knew she was dead-on. "I'll come up with something. I have to."

Chapter 6
Gage

It had been a long day, but I needed to swing by the market and pick up a frozen pizza. I would cruise by on my way home just to make sure everything looked quiet. I said good night to the desk sergeant and headed out to my truck. Once inside, I sat there for a couple of minutes in the dark, the exhaustion washing over me. There were times like this I wish I had inherited magic from Mom to have the truck drive for me. Before I could turn the engine over, I noticed Dax jog down the front steps, hop into his vehicle, and back out of the parking lot. His tires chirped the moment they touched the street. Where was he going in such a hurry?

There was only one way to find out, and I wasn't sorry to be following my newest co-worker. It wasn't that I didn't trust him, but I learned a long time ago to always follow my gut. Right now, it was pressing down on the gas.

I recognized the street he had turned down, and his car pulled into Lily's driveway. My heart quickened. Was she in danger and called Dax thinking he would come faster? The moment he parked, he crossed the deck, heading to the back door. I parked on the street, and my feet beat a quick path around the house. I gave it a rap on the back and walked in. It wasn't unusual for me to do just that, so I wasn't prepared for the shocked expression to flash over my fiancée's face.

"Gage." She crossed the room and gave me a quick hug. "What are you doing here? I figured you would go home and crash for the night."

I took in the empty pizza box on top of the trash can, two empty wine bottles, a plate with remnants of cookies, and in the center of the kitchen table were two teapots along with Lily's clue board propped open. Nikki and Mimi were there, each with a cup of tea in front of them.

"From the looks of things, missing a collaborative conversation about a potential crime." My brow cocked as I gave Dax an inquiring look. "What are you doing here?"

She placed a hand on my arm which redirected my gaze back to her.

"I called him. We weren't sure how to share what we've discovered with you. I thought bouncing everything off Dax would be beneficial for all of us."

My pride was dented that Lily would think to discuss something of this importance with Dax before me.

"Gage." Lily turned me so that I was facing her. "This isn't going to be a normal case for you, and since Dax is a witch, we—well, I—thought he could be a valuable resource."

Dax shrugged. "I'm in the dark, Gage, on what the ladies have discovered, but if this helps her and you, then I'm all in."

It was clear his loyalty to Lily was strong, and given the fact that she usually went off on her own trying to solve a puzzle, I'd rather have him around than not. And the last time, Dax was with her when she made a breakthrough on the case of the murdered leprechaun. In the overall scheme of things, it didn't matter as long as she was safe.

"Since I'm here, why don't you fill us both in and see how we can wrap up this case of the magician's murder."

She snapped her fingers. "I knew it wasn't an accident. There is no possible way that bookcase could have toppled over onto Luca."

Nikki tossed her a piece of chalk and Lily left my side to write on the board.

Luca Rand – Murder – Confirmed.

I scanned the other items listed, and now I was confused. The blood froze in my veins when I read the words break-in, home. Pointing to the chalkboard, I asked, "Lily, what does that mean? Someone broke into your house?" I could hear the growl in my voice that I used on suspects. They cowered and would tell the truth, but she wasn't the least bit put off by my tone.

"Well, this is the information I needed to figure out so that you, in turn, can spin it to Sharon and Mac."

Shaking my head and resting my forehead in the palm of my hand, I said, "Lily, the truth isn't something you spin to suit a specific narrative. The truth must stand on its own."

Dax pointed to a vacant chair. "You might want to sit down and listen to the rest of the evidence before you continue."

I had little choice but to sit down and wait for Lily to share her theory. The sound of the chair legs scraping over the wooden floor reverberated in the silence. Once seated, I leaned back, and Mimi handed me a mug of tea. But not before she added a dash of brandy to it, careful to avoid looking into my eyes.

She nodded to the cup. "You're going to need that."

I didn't like the sound of where this conversation was headed, so I took a drink and was surprised at how smooth the hot beverage was.

"I'm going to give you a quick recap—some you know, some you don't." Lily waited for me to take another sip of the tea.

"Luca and his friends were in my store yesterday, and he wanted my book, *Practical Beginnings*, which of course Milo helped me to defend until Nikki showed up. But sometime during the night, someone was able to break through my protection spell using dark magic. They took my black tourmaline necklace and the extra key I had to the store."

She held up her hand to silence me as I was gearing up to ask questions.

"Aunt Mimi detected a lingering signature for the magic. She doesn't know who it was, but only that the witch was powerful enough to get through the protections I have around the house." She glanced at Mimi who nodded.

"That's true. I protected Lily's home years ago and have, from time to time, reinforced the spells. Now that she knows how to do the spells, they're double the strength."

"Then how did they get in?" Inwardly, I shuddered to think that someone had gotten close enough to her to remove the necklace, but I didn't want to bring that up specifically.

Dax said, "Once they got inside, the rest wasn't a picnic, but it can be done. First, locating the key is first year witch training and with strong intention, removing the necklace is mid-level for someone who practices dark magic. The witch was able to get Luca in the store and plant Lily's necklace so that she would be implicated in the crime, once it was confirmed it was murder."

Lily looked at the floor, then at me. "Which it has to be, if the bolts securing the bookcases to the wall were loosened." I knew she wanted me to confirm that, but sometimes the best confirmation is not denying the truth while maintaining my professional ethics.

"Where do we start?" Nikki said.

I gestured to the chalkboard. "Bring Dax and me up to speed."

As Lily filled us in, I tried to think of a way I could spin all of this to Peabody and Mac, but everything about this case was laced with magic. If I pulled the magic out of the conversation, it might be believable that Lily hadn't noticed her necklace was gone until we found it, and when she looked for her extra store key, it was missing from her home office. That was plausible. But the bigger question was, how could I actively participate in this investigation?

Dax was listening intently, and the occasional twitch downward of his mouth indicated his growing concern for this situation. As a recent addition to our community, he wouldn't be aware of all the ins and outs of the coven my mom and Mimi belonged to. I knew by default Nikki and Lily did as well, but she had never mentioned attending a meeting. Maybe it was something she wasn't supposed to discuss with a non-magical.

"Gage." The sharpness in Lily's voice pulled my attention back to the conversation.

"Sorry. I was trying to figure out how to give information to Mac and Peabody. I can't add dark magic to the murder board at the station." It was easier to acknowledge this was a homicide investigation. Based on the heft of the bookcases they could only have been moved by one person with magic. Which Lily could have done, but she would never harm a living soul. Instinctively she knew, as had I, this wasn't an accident. Someone killed Luca Rand.

"And what did you come up with?" She pointed to my mug of tea. "Drink up, it will help with clarity."

I did as she asked and noted the hint of honey in the brew, just the way I liked it. Then it dawned on me, another layer to this investigation. I would have to excuse myself as the lead since my fiancée was about to become the prime suspect.

"Gage, what just popped into your overtaxed brain?" She smiled. "You don't need to say a word. You get this look in your eyes when you're working through a problem. We can help."

I looked from Lily to Nikki and Mimi, and then I turned to Dax.

He shifted on the chair as if he was trying to get comfortable. I wasn't looking forward to stepping aside or putting him in the hot seat. He could handle it, but I needed to be Lily's hero and solve the murder, and this time it was going to be without her help.

"What do you need me to do, Gage?" Dax asked.

"Actually, a couple of things."

"Whatever it is, consider it done."

I had known I could count on him. "I'll need for you to run the investigation, be Mac and Peabody's go-to person until we arrest the guilty party."

He gave a curt nod and remained silent, waiting for me to say whatever else had to be said, and this was going to cause me to take a big step to the sideline. "I need for you to help Lily discover who broke into her house and then her store. Other than be her sidekick, I don't have the skill set to ferret out the user of magic, dark or not."

He glanced at Lily before saying, "You can count on me."

The mood grew oppressive in the kitchen. And I only had one question left. "Is your skill level high enough to protect her should the need arise?"

Dax looked at Lily, and he leaned back in his chair. When I looked at her, I knew why he hadn't answered.

Her face was a deep red, and that meant one thing. I had gone way too far, insinuating she couldn't take care of herself, and what she was about to say was deserved. I only wanted what was best for the love of my life.

Tapping the toe of her boot on the floor, she glowered at me. "Did you forget I'm a witch, with skills of my own? And that I have a book which for some strange reason always shows me exactly what I need, when I need it?"

Stuttering, I said, "I ... um..."

"In addition, I have Nikki and Aunt Mimi who can teach me anything I might need. Plus, probably a few more witches in town, most of whom I don't even know yet, but there isn't an outside chance that I need Dax to protect me from anything. I do need his help while I search for clues, and if I learn something valuable, I'll be happy to inform him so they can follow up through the non-magical channels. But I have no intention of being a good little witch and letting others fight this battle."

Sufficiently chastised, I tipped my head to the side and looked at her. "I didn't mean to imply that you're not a strong and talented witch. I've seen what you can do that, from what my mom has told me, no first-year witch should be able to accomplish. You continue to surprise her and I'm sure your aunt."

Mimi said, "Gage. I understand your fear for what

could happen to Lily now that we've realized someone is out to frame her. But you need to understand the Michaels witches are powerful, even someone just learning. Trust in Lily's ability. We do."

Nikki and Dax nodded.

Nikki said, "If it makes you feel better, I'll spend as much time as I can with Lily so that she can practice casting spells." She looked at Dax. "Is there anything you can teach her to protect against dark magic?"

Lily smacked the tabletop. "Do you hear yourselves? You're all casting doubt on my skills to take care of myself. It stops now." She picked up the teapot and tapped the lid before waiting a moment, then poured herself a fresh cup. The steam that curled into the air was more like it had been freshly made, and that is the moment I realized she was proving a point. There was a lot she could do that I had no idea about.

She gave us all a sweet smile. "Tea, anyone?"

Dax snorted a laugh, and Nikki held out her cup. But it was Aunt Mimi's grim expression that stopped me from relaxing.

"Lily, the extent of your skills isn't the question. The worrisome factor is, how strong is the unknown witch? They broke through your protection spell on your house and walked inside. That is the one place you should always be secure."

Lily avoided Mimi's eyes as she finished pouring tea.

"Lily Michaels, please tell me this house was well protected and you reinforced the spell every week?"

"Cookies, anyone? I think I have some left over from yesterday from the Sweet Spot."

The room was so quiet you could hear a cauldron bubble from a mile away.

She threw up her hands. "I thought I only had to do it once and it was good in perpetuity. The book never said it was a weekly kind of thing like taking out the garbage."

55

Chapter 7
Lily

Nikki's mouth gaped open. Dax was shaking his head as Gage leaped up and began to pace the width of the kitchen. Aunt Mimi's eyes widened, and Milo sauntered in.

He took a look at the people gathered around my table, and with his tail flicking from side to side, asked, "What did you do now?"

"Why do you immediately assume that I have done something?" I couldn't believe Milo was so quick to be against me. He was my familiar, and I thought the code was he always had my back.

He rested on his haunches and stared at me. In a contest with my cat, I always lost, so I had given up trying. But today I wasn't going to back down. Popping my hands on my hips, I said, "Well?"

"My dear witch," he began, "I heard you mention 'the book never said' which means you've overlooked something important. Maybe it was something you and I should have discussed." As if he was already bored with our conversation, he began to lick his paw so he could wash his face.

"After all the treats I give you, I'd think you'd just volunteer information. You are supposed to be guiding me."

He cast a glance my way and continued to wash his face, but to his credit, he said, "What should I have told you?"

I folded my arms over my chest and inwardly groaned. This wasn't going to end with me getting any kind of support. I could feel it. "The house needed weekly boosts to the protection spell. And for something that important, why didn't you tell me?"

"You never asked." Now he was concentrating on the opposite foot and side of his face.

"Milo! Stop fussing over yourself and tell me what else I've overlooked. Because I didn't know, someone got into this house last night and stole a key and my protection necklace."

"I wondered how that ended up on the floor of the store, but now it makes purr-fect sense."

It was annoying when he rolled his *R*'s for the word perfect. But I wasn't about to complain. What else did I need to know? I sank to my knees and looked him in the eye. "Milo, please, if there is anything else that I should be doing, would you tell me?"

He paused in mid-swipe of his ear. "To my knowledge, there isn't anything that is lacking, and for the record, your spell wasn't that weak. But the one area you need to work on is making sure that your pendant is always protected. If that is compromised, everything is."

I scooped him up and held him to my chest. "I don't know what I'd do if something had happened to you." Then I looked at him. "Why didn't you wake me when the intruder entered the house?"

"Remember, I told you I was at a meeting."

I gave him a side-eye. "You seem to get together with your familiar friends a lot."

Aunt Mimi cleared her throat. "If you're done with Milo, can we get back to the matter at hand? We must determine how strong the unknown witch is and what their end game is."

I put Milo down and said, "It's obvious they wanted Luca out of the way for whatever reason, and pinning the crime on me keeps the focus off the real killer."

"But why?" Aunt Mimi tapped the top of the table. "What was Luca into that caused another person to wish him harm? Was he cheating someone out of money? Was it revenge, jealousy, a scorned lover?"

Gage said, "Lily mentioned that he's been in town before, and years ago, he wanted the Michaels family's book of magic. Do you think it's possible someone from the coven was trying to protect your family by getting rid of him?"

Aunt Mimi shook her head. "Everyone in our coven has taken a vow to do no harm. This would definitely violate that golden rule." She screwed up her face as she paused. "I can't think of anyone who would go against a sacred vow and risk the extreme consequences."

I shuddered, not even being able to comprehend what those might be, and sat down at the table. "Why would he have been after the book and also in the store?" I looked at Gage. "Have you searched his motel room yet?"

"Mac and Peabody did earlier and reported his room was very tidy, but there weren't any papers or items other than his clothes, costumes, and personal care items. Just as I might have expected from anyone passing through town."

"He used to be an avid reader," Mimi said. "Are you sure there weren't any books or newspapers in the room?"

"If there had been, it would have been in the report and

they also would have brought them in as potential evidence," Dax said. "Are you saying, in your opinion, that would be unusual?"

She nodded. "People don't change much, especially as we age. It was something he was passionate about. I remember he would say that reading opened doors to him that he never even dreamed were waiting for him." Her voice softened. "It was something we had in common."

I thought of a love affair which had soured. Now to bring it up after all these years must be difficult, especially since Aunt Mimi had married the love of her life almost a year ago. Not that it would be an issue with Nate, who was the most secure husband I'd seen. "If he didn't have any reading material, that would cause me to think someone took it."

Gage gave a thoughtful nod. "But with it gone, valuable clues might already have been destroyed."

I asked, "Is Monica still in the office most days or did she hire someone?" Monica Webster had purchased the motel almost two years ago now and had done a great job freshening up the place after she bought it. This time of year, guests were few and far between, but come warm weather, she'd be busy from sunrise to sunset.

Gage said, "Monica's behind the scenes, but she's hired Torrie Brooks to run the office. Why, what are you thinking?"

Things were about to get tense, so I chose my words carefully. "Maybe someone should run out to the motel in the morning, who isn't a police officer, and chat up Torrie, see if she remembers seeing anything out of the ordinary."

"And who do you think would be the likely candidate to have this conversation?"

I didn't bother to look at Gage since we both knew who I was referring to.

As if she read my mind, Nikki said, "I don't have any plans in the morning, so Lily and I will run out there and see what we can uncover."

Resisting the urge to slap her a high five, I gave Gage and then Dax a sweet, innocent smile. "If we learn anything worthwhile, I'll be sure to fill you both in."

Gage tapped his fingertips together, not that weighing the pros and cons would change our minds. Short of being locked up in jail, we'd be on the road by eight and talking to Torrie by eight fifteen.

He gave Dax a side-glance. "What do you think?"

He shook his head. "I'm not getting in the middle of you two, but looking at this from a purely investigative point of view, Lily has an amazing track record for uncovering critical details, and as long as she promises to share with us what they learn and she enhances her self-protection spell, I see no reason why she shouldn't talk with Torrie. A friendly face is more apt to get information that we can't."

Mimi said, "I'll come by in the morning with a new pendant which should put your mind at ease, Gage."

Finally, my people were starting to see my side of this problem, and supporting me following the clues was immensely gratifying. "Gage, I will be fine." I did a little jig in my chair. "And don't forget, I've got skills most people only dream of having."

He chuckled. "That doesn't make me feel any better. All it does is remind me you can be a tad reckless when you're following clues."

I sat up straight and said in a clear, firm voice, "Actually, that's not true. I stopped looking for danger after Nikki and

I were almost caught spying on Teddy Roberts. Remember, when I was following up on who killed Flora Gray?"

He looked at Dax. "This is why I don't encourage Lily and Nikki to hunt for clues."

In his slow Southern drawl, Dax said, "Try a different perspective. We know where they're going and when. If there's trouble, we don't have to figure out where they are, so it's much safer than Lily deciding to go off and not tell anyone where she is."

My head bobbed like one of those little dolls on a dashboard. "See, Dax understands."

"I'm still not a fan, but there is some kind of weird logic to it all." He placed his hand on top of mine. "I want you to promise me if you get any of that witchy intuition telling you to get out of that office, listen to the voice and come back to town. And no knocking on doors."

I watched him swallow, and I knew that lump in his throat was a sign of how he felt about me. But I had to follow the clues where they led. My life and freedom were on the line, and if it wasn't for Gage running the investigation and now Dax, I probably would have already been questioned, if not arrested on suspicion of murder. This time around, the stakes were higher, and I knew it was going to get worse before it got better.

"Gage, when you talked with Luca's partners, did any of them have anything of interest to say? Like who they thought might be the guilty party?"

His casual demeanor changed, and he studied the floor with great interest. "That is an official police conversation that I'm not at liberty to discuss."

"Bat tails."

Aunt Mimi's head snapped up. She had never heard that tone of voice come out of my mouth.

"They pointed their little magician fingers in my direction, and you don't want to tell me."

His eyes bored into mine. I could see the anguish in them, and a chill raced over my body. That is exactly what happened, and he was doing all he could to protect me. I lowered my voice. "They did, didn't they?"

His head bobbed once, and the room was silent for a few moments. I pushed the chair back and stood. "Then it makes even more sense that Nikki and I will be following the clue tomorrow to wherever it might lead."

"There's nothing I can do to change your mind, Lily?"

Gage looked at me with such intensity I wished I could tell him what he wanted to hear, but I wasn't about to start evading the truth now to make it easier for him or anyone.

"Don't ask me that. Do you think this is easier when other people's futures were on the line? This is me, and I won't sit on the sidelines while someone out there is methodically planning on framing me for a crime I didn't commit."

He turned his attention to Mimi. "You'll help her increase the protection spell?"

Aunt Mimi gave me a small, comforting smile. "Of course, I will."

Nikki said, "And now that I'm home, I've reclaimed my role as Lily's trusty sidekick, Watson."

He gave her a small smile, but it didn't reach his eyes. "And Dax and I will follow up on what we can do. Tomorrow, we'll be back at the shop, and with any luck, I can turn the Cozy Nook back over to you in thirty-six hours."

Even if I had wanted to protest, I wouldn't. Gage and everyone on the police force would be doing their best to finish scouring the scene. "Do me one favor. Will you and Dax take a close look at the bolts that secured the bookcase to the wall? Neither Mac nor Sharon would be able to tell if it was magic that seared them, but you will since you know that is a possibility."

Dax said, "We should get there early. I can cast a spell that would be able to help with that, but I can't do it if the others are around."

Nodding, Gage said, "We should meet at seven. And I'll tell Mac and Peabody we wanted to get in and out of the shop before lookie-loos came out of the woodwork. I don't want to cast any more suspicion on Lily if it can be helped."

Now the guys were getting on board. "What else should we be looking for tomorrow?" I snapped my fingers. "We can stop at the theatre. Alfred will know the details about the show and if it will even happen now that their lead act is unable to perform."

Nikki asked, "How do you know he was the lead?"

I dropped my chin and gave her a sharp look. "Really, by the way those other three seemed to defer to him while in the shop? It's the only logical choice."

"You're right." She pushed back her chair. "I hate to cut this short, but Steve is probably wondering why I'm running late."

I went around the table and gave her a hug. "Tell him I'm sorry about keeping his new bride here, and next time when he's done with work, he needs to swing over. The door is always open." I glanced at Aunt Mimi. "But it will be better protected after today."

She threw her arms around my neck and held me tight. "I'll be over bright and early, ready to crack the case."

Laughing, I hugged her back. "I'm not sure we'll solve it tomorrow, but it will be the first proactive step we've taken, so we're closer to solving the puzzle."

She pointed to my board. "Don't forget to take a picture

before you put it away for the night. With some unknown witch roaming the streets of Pembroke Cove able to cast strong spells, we don't want to take any chances with that information getting into the wrong hands."

"Unless they can read through walls, we're safe." I was still laughing as the smile slipped from my face when she clasped my hands in hers.

"Lily, do not underestimate this person."

Aunt Mimi got up and wrapped her arms around us both. Together they began to speak in a soft soothing tone. Dax held his hands, palms up, from the other side of the table and closed his eyes. Gage placed his right hand over his heart. It was with that final gesture that I knew I had been surrounded with love which was the greatest protection of all.

Chapter 8
Lily

The next morning, I was wide awake and ready to go by seven. I hadn't slept well, tossing and turning, so I had opened up my book of spells. The pages had flipped open, providing a spell on how to defend against dark magic. But without being able to actually practice the spell, to see if it worked, I would be flying in the dark if, or when, I had to use it. The incantation tumbled over in my brain as I continued to repeat the words like a mantra, hoping it became a reflex much like most of my other spells had.

A tap on the door drew me to see who was stopping by so early. "Aunt Mimi." I opened the door wider.

My aunt swept into the room, and dangling from her fingertips was a chain and a stone at the end. "I want you to wear this until your protection necklace is returned to you." She slipped it over my head and placed her hand over the stone, her mouth moving, but I couldn't hear the words. She then kissed my cheek and patted the other one. "I'm off." The door closed behind her before I could say a word.

. . .

Twas sitting at the kitchen table sipping coffee when Milo stalked in, grumbling about the early hour and the noise of my banging cabinet doors. I think he was secretly pleased about my proactive approach. Nikki and I were going to talk to Torrie, and hopefully Monica, at the motel and see what we could learn about the four magicians who had come to town.

He nodded at the necklace. "I see your aunt was here."

"For all of one minute. She breezed in, placed the necklace on me, said a few words, and left."

"Busy witch."

He trotted out the kitty door, leaving me to my thoughts as they drifted to Iris and the way she reacted in the shop when she saw my book of magic. It seemed that was the sole purpose for coming into the store which made sense after Aunt Mimi had said he wanted to get his hands on that book years ago. I had been surprised to learn real magicians, not like the kind who pull fake flowers out of their sleeves, aren't born with magic like witches. They have to study and learn how to do spells along with sleight of hand and persuade people to believe what they're seeing. As it's been said many times, seeing is believing, and that is the real magic. Someone like Luca Rand would have practiced until he was flawless.

Could he have discovered a way to get the pages in my book, *Practical Beginnings*, to be visible to him? That was a thread that needed to be tugged, and possibly, it would unravel a bit more of this mystery.

Milo bumped against my leg, breaking me out of the thoughts swirling in my brain. "Are we having breakfast before we go to the motel?"

My brows shot to my hairline. "You're going with us?"

"I thought I would." He hopped into my lap and sat

down and began to knead his claws into the leg of my jeans. "I know you and Nikki are tough, but I feel responsible that someone got into the house when I wasn't home. If I had been, things might have been different and there wouldn't be a cloud of suspicion hanging over your head right now."

Placing a kiss on the top of his soft gray head, I said, "Milo, I don't blame you. If anyone is at fault, it's me. I should have asked more about the protection spell. You have no reason to feel anything other than relief that we're unharmed."

He tipped his head to the side and gave me an assessing look. "You're right. Next time, ask more questions about your spells and how effective they are for what length of time. It's an important tidbit. In all instances."

There was my snarky feline. Quick to let me take the full weight of wrongdoing, but I was to blame, not Milo. I set him on the chair and moved to the pantry. Getting his can of wet food, I didn't bother to look at the clue board. Nothing had changed since last night. Nor would it until after we talked with the ladies at the motel.

I closed the pantry door a little harder than I needed to and with each step to the counter, my frustration bubbled up. I smacked the can on the counter, yanked a bowl out of the cupboard, and banged the cabinet door closed.

"Are you going to keep slamming things until something breaks?"

I whirled around and glared at Milo. "What are you talking about?"

"You forget, my dear witch, I have spent several years observing you, long before you knew I could talk. And when you're upset or frustrated, you bang doors, books on tables, bowls on counters." He tipped his head, and I swear he winked at me. "Shall I go on?"

"Do you think by looking all cute and being sweet, you can get me out of this mood?"

He grumbled, "The one that's settled over you like thick pea soup fog in the harbor?" He looked at the bowl and can on the counter. "Any chance we can have breakfast and talk about it?"

I felt my lips quirk into a smile. "You want to talk through the case?"

"After I eat, yes. I think better on a full stomach."

I opened the can, scooped the food into a bowl, and placed it on the chair next to him. I figured since he was in the mood to be helpful, I'd serve breakfast to him so he didn't have to get down to get it. Not that across the kitchen was far, but hey, I was accommodating as well as grouchy.

He purred his contentment as he seemed to inhale his seafood feast. I poured myself another mug of coffee, grateful I had remembered to make a full pot. It was going to be that kind of a day. Milo paused and looked at me.

"You should make some toast or something. Sleuthing is fueled by brain power, and the brain is fueled by energy. Food is energy." He turned his attention back to his breakfast.

I hated to admit he was right. I functioned better on a full stomach, and I didn't understand how people could just have black coffee for breakfast either. This was when being a kitchen witch would come in handy. With a flick of a wrist and strong intentions, and of course a good spell, I could be enjoying a healthy home-cooked breakfast, instead of a bowl of Toasted O's and a banana. I got up and at the same time, I sighed.

Without looking up, Milo paused. "You can use your powers to do some basic kitchen witch spells. It is a learned practice, not innate."

"How did you...?" My words trailed off. Not asking Milo a dumb question was in my best interest to avoid another snarky comment. He sat back, and his tail swished first right and then left. Too late.

"Why do you always underestimate my ability to know exactly what you're thinking?"

"To think you can read my mind is unnerving." My retort was quick and didn't faze him in the least as he continued to study me.

"For the record, I don't read your mind."

If a cat could shudder like a human, he would have. "That's a relief."

"However," he purred, "spending as much time together as we do and will for the rest of your life, I've come to learn how your mind works, much like before when I knew you were upset because you bang things. Think of it like this: you can anticipate what Gage or Nikki are thinking most of the time, correct?"

I leaned against the counter and slowly nodded my head. "True."

"Good, now that we have that established, we can move on. Pour yourself some of those tasteless O's you love so much, and we can get down to what we really must focus on —who is out to frame you for the murder of Luca Rand."

Milo was perched on the edge of the chair, studying the clue board. My cereal bowl and a darkening banana peel were on the table, pushed aside for now.

Nikki opened the back door and came in holding a cake platter in one hand and an oversized tote bag in the other. "Good morning. I hope you're hungry. I wanted to try a new coffee cake recipe, and since you're always so gracious to give me honest feedback, I brought it along." She grinned as she let the sentence hang. "What are you two doing?" She placed the cake plate in the middle of the table and the bag next to a vacant chair.

Milo said, "We've been talking about dark magic and who could have cast the spell. And as I was about to tell Lily, I think one of the remaining three magicians is a witch."

It was handy that all witches could understand when a familiar was talking—at least the witches I knew understood Milo. I picked up the chalk to make a note. His explanation resonated with me, but I was still unclear on one point. "Why does that make a difference?"

"Dark magic is very hard to master, contrary to what some witches would want you to believe. It takes determination and effort to manifest their dark side and then harness the energy to cast a spell."

"More powerful than Aunt Mimi?"

Nikki nodded. "I've heard stories from my family about a rogue witch who dove into the dark side. If this person is skilled, like Milo has said, they can be very powerful. However, a pure and passionate heart, like Mimi's, can prevail in the end. We need to believe in the power of good over evil."

"Sounds like something from a nursey rhyme."

Milo cocked his head and looked between Nikki and me. "Where do you think they originated from? Everything is based in history. Now, some have taken liberties with the truth, but trust me, facts are facts."

I sank into my chair. Every time I thought I couldn't be surprised by our heritage, something new cropped up. But I guess it made sense that all stories were based on something.

"Let's get back to the problem at hand instead of me diving into a rabbit hole on the history of witches."

"Agreed." Nikki nodded and glanced at Milo. "We need to hit the road and see what we can learn from Monica and Torrie, and with any luck, we might run into three magicians, aka the three suspects."

I knew she was right; they were the only logical people who could have killed Luca, but it chilled me to the bone that someone he thought was a friend and co-worker had lured him to his death. I sat up straighter. That was something that hadn't fully formed until this instant. "Luca had to have been the intended victim all along, and one of them is the guilty party. I'll bet it's Iris."

"Why her and not the other two?" Milo asked.

"She was the most aggressive at the shop, as if she was Luca's right-hand person. Clay and Celeste were quieter and seemed to defer to Luca."

"But that breeds resentment in others. Taking a back seat to someone is hard to swallow for most." Nikki pointed to the chalkboard. "You need to write her name down in the suspect column. Maybe if we get lucky, or by your amazing skill, we'll have more details to add when we get back."

I jumped up and clapped my hands together, hoping to get some energy going in our trio. Milo had lost his snark, and Nikki just looked worried. I knew the idea of dark magic gave me pause, and it had them as well. But there was no way we could solve the puzzle without more pieces. "Let's hit the road." With a forced smile plastered on my face, I was determined to stay upbeat.

Nikki grabbed her bag and looked longingly at the cake. "When we get back, I'm slicing into that, and we are eating a big piece."

I looped my arm through Nikki's. "I was thinking of

having two." Squeezing her arm tight, I guided her to the door as Milo slipped ahead of us and out the little kitty door I had installed just for him.

She looked at me. "Are you nervous?"

Shaking my head, I said, "Not at all. With the two of us together, our magic is unbeatable."

Under her breath, she said, "I'd prefer we didn't have to find out."

After a short drive to the motel, I parked in a space close to the sign that said Office. Milo had ridden in Nikki's lap.

I gave his ears a scratch. "Are you staying in the car?"

"How am I supposed to slink around and search for clues sitting in here where I could take a nice catnap?"

If a cat could roll his eyes to highlight how annoyed he was, Milo would be the poster kitty. "Fine. I'll put the window down so when you're done, we'll meet you back here."

"Excellent idea." He head-bumped my hand. "Now be careful, and if you need me, you know what to do."

"I've got Nikki with me, but thank you for your concern." I glanced at the office, unsure what we were about to walk into, but I was confident that with my best friend by my side, I could conquer whatever it was. I pushed the window button, and it slid down.

"Just doing my job, my dear witch." He pushed himself off Nikki's lap, walked across mine, and hopped up onto the window opening. "I just had a thought. Since the two of you are having cake, what's going to be my treat when we get home?"

"Oh, Milo, do you always think of your stomach first and potential danger second?"

He tapped his paw to my arm. "A familiar is rarely in danger, especially since cats are most often overlooked by humans."

Now that made me feel bad since I'm sure he was right with that statement. Dogs, people stooped to pet and make a fuss over, but cats not as much, unless of course you were like me and loved all animals. "I'll open up a can of salmon as a special snack."

"Well, if that's the best you can do." He hopped to the ground and trotted down the walkway, headed to heaven only knew where.

Nikki was laughing quietly.

I turned and gave her a quick look. "What's so funny?"

"You and Milo banter like you've been doing the witch and familiar relationship for years, not months. It's just good to see, that's all."

"I'll deny if you ever tell him, but I love that little smoked salmon-loving cat with every fiber of my soul."

Her grin grew until it filled her face. "That is exactly how this relationship should be." Putting her hand on the door handle, she said, "Ready to start being an ace detective?"

I tipped my head. "I prefer to be referred to as super-sleuth and you as my Watson."

She laughed out loud and clapped her hands together. "Lily, you are too funny."

Bobbing my head toward the office, I said, "Let's hope the ladies in there find me so quirky that they tell me every detail they know about our traveling magicians." With that, I pushed open the door and closed it with a bang.

Chapter 9
Gage

Dax and I walked into the Cozy Nook Bookshop before nine the next morning. As Lily had asked, the first thing I wanted to check out were the bolts that should have anchored the bookcases securely to the wall. Peabody and Mac were going to talk with Alfred Schwartz at the Lights Out Theatre to follow up on who booked them and for how long. It wasn't like Pembroke Cove often had these types of shows before the summer season was in full swing.

With a snap of his fingers, the overhead lights came on, adding a harsh glow to the bright yellow crime scene tape that fluttered in the breeze from the open door. It was the first time I had seen Dax use his magic on the job.

"I'm going to check the back door." He strode across the room, disappearing into the small kitchen which doubled as Lily's office and storage room.

I hesitated, wanting to examine the bolts, but since Dax was now the lead on the case, I should wait for him. I didn't want there to be any doubt about the chain of evidence in this case. So, I cooled my heels and stayed rooted to the spot where I had the best view of the store and out the windows, the two huge panes of glass, one that faced the street and the other that was in clear line of sight for the alleyway. At this time of day, no one had come out yet. At least except for the tradesmen that were headed into Tucker's Hardware.

How I wished that this was a normal day and Lily would be arriving soon and would be handling a cup of coffee and something mouthwateringly good from the Sweet Spot. But that would have to wait at least one, if not several, more days.

Dax returned. "All clear back there. No one tried to gain access overnight."

"That's a relief."

"And I added a little something extra to protect against unlawful entry with any key other than one that is in Lily's hand or ours."

I nodded, grateful that he was able to add a little something extra. Half in jest, I said, "Any way to add an alert if someone tries? Like you know on home security cameras it shows up on a cell phone."

"Gage, trust me. If someone tries to break through my magic, I'll know it."

His face was devoid of any expression. I thought of it as his federal face—never betray any emotion, good or bad. And I did trust him. After all, he had saved Lily's life last fall and had put himself in the line of danger a few more times since then. I trusted Dax like I never had anyone before him, and that was saying a lot since Mac had been beside me since my early days as a police officer. "Where should we start?" I redirected my attention back to the task at hand. We had to uncover clues about what really had happened here.

"Do we have a time of death?" Dax stepped over scattered books and moved along the aisle to where the bookcase should be secured to the wall.

"Let me check my email." As he was climbing on a small stool that Lily must use when putting books on the shelf, I tapped the screen on my phone. I scrolled through the messages in my inbox and located what I needed. "It says here he died around five in the morning, and this is interesting." I paused to read a little further in the message. "It says the alcohol in his blood was off the charts. So not only did the guy break in to try and steal Lily's book, but he was snockered as well."

He chuckled. "Is that the word of the day?"

I looked up from the screen. "It's not one that can easily be woven into a sentence, but it fits the context."

Dax got down from the stool, and it wobbled from side to side. He righted himself and then made his way back to the open space. "The bolts were unscrewed from the walls, not cut, which confirms my suspicion that they were magically loosened." He opened his gloved hand, and resting in the palm was a bolt that, other than plaster dust, was in perfect condition.

"How long does it take to work that kind of spell?"

He turned it over and peered at the opposite side. "By the condition of this, not long." Looking at me, he said, "I don't know how we'll record this for the official report. I'm sure Mac and Peabody will even wonder when they look at the pictures I took of the bolts resting on the edge of the holes in the wall."

I understood exactly what he meant. "Why wasn't this on the shelf that was upright? If it was loosened, it would have dropped there or maybe even to the floor. Three four-foot sections are secured together with the bolt."

He shook his head. "You're forgetting that Mimi owned

this store first. My guess is she reinforced the shelves with magic, but once Lily took over, those spells weakened since she didn't know that she needed to."

I nodded. "Just like her house."

"Exactly." Dax moved around to where the top of the bookcase was propped up at an awkward angle from removing Luca Rand. "Here's what I'm picturing."

I recognized his posture as he rested his hand on his chin, contemplating the scene and organizing his thoughts. It was similar to mine when I was mulling things over on a case.

"Our perp entered Lily's house at some point around midnight and took the key and necklace from her. Then it was preplanned for Luca and whoever the other person was to enter the bookshop and search for the book."

"Why would he think the book would be in the shop and not at her house? If whoever it was searched her place, they would have found it and could have taken it at that point."

He glanced my way and then back to where Luca had been found. "The book is the cover. I'd bet my wand it was never about the Michaels's magic book—well, except for our victim; he wanted it. The intent was to kill Rand and make it look like Lily had done it after finding him in her book-shop. She gets angry, maybe there's even a struggle, the pendant was torn from her neck and landed unseen near the body. In anger she pushed over the bookcase, crushing Luca. Then she goes home and pretends to find him a few hours later."

"And when they took the necklace, could they have added a twist to the spell so she wouldn't have realized it was gone?"

The corners of Dax's mouth tipped down. "Yes. I'm

sure that's what happened. If I had dipped my toe into that black magic cauldron, it's what I would have done. If Lily had noticed it was missing, she would have spent time looking for it, then the time between the accident and Lily getting to her store would have widened."

A finger of fear ran down my spine. "I don't like how this sounds. The entire incident, if it happened the way you surmise, is cunning and calculated."

"We need to put the magic aside and look at this as Peabody or Mac would. How can we explain the things we believe are the result of a spell?"

I threw up my hands. "I have no idea. The bolts, the key, the necklace. I can't think of a logical explanation except the key could be explained as if Lily had misplaced it. But bolts are either cut or they grow loose over time and the weight of the bookcase would have caused them to bend slowly as they came out of the wall."

"But they're pristine. And you confirmed that she was wearing the necklace during your date in front of them so we can't pass it off that she must have dropped it before leaving the store."

Hanging my head, I said, "I wish I had thought before shooting off my mouth. It's my fault the guilty finger is pointing directly at her."

He crossed the room and clapped a hand on my shoulder. "Don't blame yourself. All you did was answer a question. In that split second, there was no way you could have seen the implications."

Logically, he was right, but she was my fiancée. I should be protecting her. Now Dax was trying to find a way to shift the focus from Lily to an unknown person. "Is there anything else we can learn from the shop at this point? I think we should meet up with Peabody and Mac to see what they learned from Alfred about the upcoming show."

Dax said, "Good idea. I'm going to secure the front door like I did the back, just to make sure whoever has that key doesn't come around. Once we get the bookcase upright, with any luck we may discover something worth finding. And we should plan on doing that later today."

"We'll bring Peabody and Mac back after lunch."

He nodded. "Sounds like we have a solid plan of attack."

I opened the door and stepped into the sunshine, but it didn't warm the inner chill I felt. For the first time in my career, I felt as if my skills as a cop weren't going to be enough to save the woman I loved from being charged with murder.

Dax pointed up the street as Peabody and Mac hurried in our direction. Hopefully, they would have information about the upcoming magician show.

When they got within hearing distance, I asked, "How did you make out?"

Mac gave me a thumbs-up, then a thumbs-down. That wasn't encouraging. I steeled myself for bad news.

Peabody looked up and down the sidewalk. There were a few people milling about, and she said, "Let's go inside the bookstore and talk."

Dax opened the door and ushered us inside. Once the door was closed, Peabody and Mac looked at the propped up bookcase. She asked, "Were the bolts cut?"

Shaking his head, Dax said, "No. It looks as if they were unscrewed."

"How could someone have removed the bolts with Luca in the building? He would have been sure to notice. Unless they did it first and he came later."

"Or," Mac interjected, "it might have been part of a vandalism plot and it was an accident?"

I thought it was interesting he was trying to be optimistic. "If that is the explanation, why didn't they call it in and report that someone was trapped under the shelf? That points to deliberate."

"They might have been scared. After all, they were breaking and entering and that is a crime." Mac was doing his best to play devil's advocate.

"It's something to consider. We'll add these details to the crime board at the station."

Peabody gave Mac a pointed look as if to tell him to stop with the accidental stuff even though I knew Mac was trying to redirect the attention away from Lily. It was something I wanted to do too, but at this point, as far as they knew, removing the bolts would have taken more time, if done the non-magical way.

Dax gave me a pointed look. He wanted to know what they had learned at the theatre.

"What did Alfred Schwartz have to say?" As I spoke, Dax focused his attention on Peabody.

She said, "It was interesting but not overly helpful. Mr. Schwartz said that he didn't book the magicians to have a show at the Lights Outs and when they showed up saying they would be performing, he was shocked. Especially since he's the main office person. He had no record of a show or even any phone calls, letters, or emails between him and the group."

"So, it's a ruse?"

"Well, not quite." Mac said, "Once they talked, Alfred

agreed they could put on a show, but he wasn't responsible for attendance. He said they were happy with the arrangement and felt confident they'd perform to a packed house."

"Were those Mr. Schwartz's exact words or someone from the group?" Dax asked.

"Alfred said that is what Luca Rand told him when they shook on the deal."

Peabody nodded. "It didn't seem like they protested much about having a contract. It was almost as if they were happy to get the gig at all."

"Which gives them a legitimate reason for being in Pembroke Cove and the opportunity to try and steal Lily's family history book."

Peabody tapped her index finger on her chin. "That's a part of this that I don't understand. What is it about that old book that would make someone want to steal it? Family history is usually important only to the family." Her eyes brightened. "Unless maybe one of the magicians thought they were a long-lost Michaels and the truth would be revealed by reading it."

That was an interesting point. "Neither Lily nor Mimi mentioned that could be a possibility. But Mimi said she dated Rand years ago, and even then, Luca wanted the book."

Peabody gave a low whistle. "There must be something pretty special about that dusty old book."

I controlled a smile and saw Dax look away as if he was doing the same. Being a witch, he'd understand how important the book was. And if either Lily or Mimi had heard Peabody refer to *Practical Beginnings* as an old dusty book, they might just put a hex on her. Well, other than the fact most witches had a *do no harm* rule, and I knew for a fact that the Michaels witches would never break that guiding principle.

Mac said, "Did you discover anything new this morning?"

Dax deferred the question to me with a nod of his head. "Other than the time of death was at five in the morning and the bolts were unscrewed, no."

"Doesn't give us much to go on," he said and Mac quickly agreed.

"We've been up against tougher cases, and we've never left one unsolved. We're not about to now, being this is Lily. We all know there is no way that sweet woman would harm a fly. Heck, I've seen her scoop up a spider and put it out her door instead of squashing it."

My heart flipped over in my chest. I should have known that Mac and Peabody would be in Lily's corner, just as Dax was as well. I clapped a hand on Mac's shoulder. "Thanks for your support. It's good to know that we all believe in Lily's innocence."

Chapter 10
Lily

As we entered the motel office, Torrie was behind the desk, frowning at the computer screen. When she finally looked up, a smile replaced her scowl.

"Lily, Nikki, this is a surprise. Welcome."

"Hi, Torrie, it's good to see you." I looked around the tidy lobby, curious if on the off chance Iris, Celeste, or Clay were hanging around. But no such luck. "I was wondering if we could talk to you for a couple of minutes about the four people who checked into the motel in the last few days."

She nodded and grinned. "I wondered when you'd come around. This is about those magicians, isn't it, and one of them died in your bookstore?"

"Guilty as charged." I flashed her what I hoped was a disarming smile. "You can imagine I have a few questions."

She stood up. "Want some coffee?" Nodding to the coffee pot across the lobby, she said, "It's fresh."

Nikki snapped her fingers. "In the car, I have just the treat to go with that."

She gave me a sly wink and headed out the door. It was only moments later she returned carrying the cake plate she had brought to my house just a short while earlier. I suppressed a grin. It was easy for her to conjure up a cake from this distance. I had to know her secret, and we'd be chatting about this on the way home.

Torrie looked at the cake and smacked her lips with a chuckle. "Now we're talking." She picked up the desk phone. "I'll let Monica know. She won't want to miss this cake, especially since Nikki baked it."

I knew exactly what she meant, and my hips showed I enjoyed her baking often. Maybe it was time to start jogging with Gage, but that idea was fleeting, just like it was each time I thought of it. I should start walking more; that would be effective too.

Torrie said, "All right, see you soon." After she hung up the phone, she came around the side of the desk. "Monica is upstairs in the apartment and will be down in a few minutes. She asked if we'd wait for her. She thought it would be more efficient if we all compared notes together. Get right to the heart of your visit."

I wondered if those were Monica's words or Torrie's, but it didn't matter. They knew why Nikki and I came out to the motel today. As I had solved a few murders in town, and now that it looked as if I was the only real suspect in a suspicious death, of course I'd be tracking down clues. What self-respecting puzzle master would leave this one alone?

Nikki said, "Lily, can you run back out to the car and grab the paper plates? I just realized I forgot them." She bobbed her head in the direction of the window, and I could see Celeste was strolling in the direction of the beach across the street. If I hurried, I could get in a few questions and be back before Monica arrived.

"Right." I zipped out the door and picked up my pace to a jog across the blacktop parking lot.

"Celeste." She slowed her steps and turned. Her over-sized sunglasses obscured her eyes, but it couldn't hide the smirk and then frown on her lips.

She crossed her arms over her chest and cocked her hip. "Well, if it isn't the little witch who killed my dear friend."

I took the little witch comment as a reference to actually being one and not that she thought I was a vile person. But who knows how she really meant it. "I'm glad I found you." My breathing was more like a wheeze from the jog, and I took deep breaths. It was easy to see she was less than thrilled to see me.

"The detective in charge of the murder you committed asked us—me, Iris, and Clay—not to leave town for a few days. Which is fine since the show must go on even if Luca had a good chunk of time being the front man."

I heard a distinct tone of disdain in her voice and there, I thought, could be a motive for Celeste to have pushed a bookcase over onto him. But I needed to know how well practiced she was in the art of magic. "I'm glad you're able to restructure the show. I'm sure there are a lot of people in town who are looking forward to going." I crossed my fingers behind my back, hoping it held at least a grain of truth.

She perked up a bit. "That is good news. I'll have to tell the others. Clay's been worried we'd perform to an empty theatre."

"And what about Iris? Was she concerned?"

"I have no idea what she's thinking. Ever since Luca died, she's been acting like she's running the show." With a snort, she continued. "As if Luca passed her the mantle of head magician or something."

The sarcasm dripped from her voice and I discerned she was less than thrilled with Iris's heavy hand in things, if that was in fact an accurate statement. But I needed to ask questions about the morning of the break-in at the store and how good Celeste was at magic, real magic, not like what magicians typically did on stage with pulling rabbits from a top hat or flowers from their sleeve.

"Have you been with the group long?"

Her brow cocked. "Is that a trick question?"

I couldn't afford to get her in defensive mode. I made sure my tone of voice was friendly and not like I was drilling her for information. "No. I was curious how you all met and if you've been working together a long time."

Her face softened. "We all met almost ten years ago at a magician school in California. Luca had big dreams that our show would eventually be picked up by a venue in Vegas."

"But you, Iris, and Clay are much younger than him." It was a statement, not a question, that I found odd. If Luca had already been saying he was a magician, why would he have gone to school a decade ago?

She gave a small laugh. "He was our teacher, not a student. Clay and Iris were dating at the time and on a lark, they came to the school. I was failing as an actress and thought if I could beef up my resume with some magic, it might be easier to get cast in roles."

"Did it work with your movie career?" I also found it very interesting that Clay and Iris were a couple; they certainly hadn't given off that vibe.

"After I started to hone my skills, Luca suggested we take our act on the road as a foursome. It was a great idea, until now." Her mouth formed a thin, hard line. "We were working our way east, and Luca wanted to wrap up in this rinky-dink little town, but we should never have come here. Iris tried to talk him out of it, but he was convinced he needed to run into his old girlfriend who owned the local bookshop. And then we met you."

She turned on her heel, and I knew she was ready to put this conversation behind her. I reached out to stop her, but she shrugged off my hand like it was an ant getting flicked away from a picnic basket.

"Do I need to call the police and report you for harassment?"

"No. But you didn't give me a chance to express my sincere condolences for your loss."

She barked, "Ha, you shouldn't bother. You had to have known Luca wouldn't have given up until he got his hands on your family's book of spells." With a flash of superiority, she continued. "I know you are a real witch, and maybe it's time someone takes you down a peg or three." And then she smirked. "And maybe that time is now." With a flutter of her fingers that was less than friendly, she strode through the parking lot, leaving me standing with more questions than answers. But I had learned one thing. Coming to Pembroke Cove was deliberate, and more than likely Luca had recruited these three people because one of them had more talent than he possessed. Now to keep digging and find out which one.

When I walked back to the office, Nikki was sitting in one of the upholstered side chairs. Torrie was pouring mugs of coffee, and Monica was slicing the cake and placing it on actual glass plates.

"Oh good, you have plates." I gave Nikki a sheepish smile, momentarily forgetting she had sent me outside on a ruse to get paper ones.

Monica handed me a plate and Torrie began passing out

mugs of hot coffee. I thanked them both and sat down next to Nikki.

Monica looked up through her lashes and gave me a knowing smile. "I see you bumped into Ms. Jaden while you were outside."

"It wasn't all rainbows and unicorns. But I learned a few things that are worth mulling over." I took the empty seat next to Nikki and accepted the cup of coffee from Torrie. "I was hoping you would answer a few questions about the four performers."

Monica gave Torrie a quick look and said, "Yes. Of course, but I don't think Torrie and I have much to share. They keep to themselves and we haven't seen them except as they walk through the parking lot." She looked at Torrie. "I don't mean to speak for you, but I just figured you haven't seen them much either."

"No," Torrie drawled out. "Not much and I'm not always at the desk, but the other night when the office was closed and I was working on the new reservation system, I saw the redhead leave and come back, and then the brunette did the same about a half hour after that, and then the two men left together."

That was before Luca was killed. "Do you remember what night that was? Could it have been the first night they checked in? And now that I think about it, when did they arrive in town?"

Torrie said, "Five nights. I know because the women came in and said they needed to extend their stay until she, the killer, was brought to justice."

"Oh." The air went out of my sail as I realized they were referring to me.

Nikki said, "Don't go there. You know you didn't do

anything to hurt Luca Rand other than say no to selling him an old book."

Monica's face perked up. "An old book. I overheard them talking, and he said the most important task he had in town was leaving with it in his possession."

Now that was very interesting. The man had been determined. I asked, "Do you remember what the others said in response to that?"

She shook her head. "Not really. I was putting bags of ice in the machine and they were walking away from me at the time, in the direction of their rooms."

"What about Clay Proctor? Did he come in and request to extend his stay too?" Nikki asked.

Torrie frowned. "Not directly. The ladies did that for him. I figured since they were all traveling together, it made sense."

"Monica, is there any chance we could get a peek inside Luca's room?" I knew it was a big ask, but there had to be something that the police had overlooked. After all, three of the four officers were non-magical and wouldn't know what they were looking at.

"I wish I could, Lily, but Dax Peters came out and asked if he could put a special lock on the room to keep it secure while they were investigating."

I kept myself from frowning, even though I knew that meant he had used magic to lock the room, not just to keep the perp from destroying any potential evidence, but I was sure it would keep me and Nikki out too. "It's okay. It didn't hurt to ask."

I took a sip of my coffee and let my mind wander as to how I was going to get inside that room. Maybe there was a spell I could cast that would be like a crystal ball and give me access. But if it was something I should be able to do, my book, *Practical Beginnings*, would have shown me.

Nikki put the cake plate in front of me. "Care for a slice?"

To be polite, I forked a piece onto the small plate she handed to me. All I really wanted to do was finish up the conversation, go find Milo, and get back to my place to write down the scant information I had uncovered. One thing that stuck out at this moment in my mind was all three of them were prime suspects.

I took a nibble of the cake and my taste buds wept in thanks. "Nikki, this pound cake is amazing, so buttery."

She grinned. "Oh, good. So I should add it to my list of available options?"

"Are you kidding? Your customers will go nuts for this."

Monica took another bite and smiled. "If I had a restaurant attached to the motel, you'd be doing all my baking. There is no way that anything which came out of my kitchen could come close."

I couldn't help but chuckle. "Yours would be much better than mine. Why do you think Nikki's my best friend? She keeps me supplied with baked goods."

I glanced through the glass door and noticed Milo was sitting on the hood of my Mini Coop, swishing his tail with exaggerated jerky movements. I winked at Nikki who seemed like she didn't notice as she continued the conversation about what other baked goods she was thinking of trying out.

"If you need unbiased taste testers, Torrie and I would be happy to run an extra mile or two just to volunteer."

Torrie's head snapped in Monica's direction. "Speak for yourself. If I needed to run five extra miles, it would be worth it."

I drained my coffee cup and stacked the plate, fork, and cup together on the small table. How was I going to get Nikki's attention when she was happily talking baking? It was going to take a minute or two. Once she got on a roll, it could be tough since she was passionate about cakes and cookies. But from the corner of my eye, I could see Milo now pacing the hood of my car. There was no doubt he had discovered a tidbit or two. And if they were really good, there was a fishy treat on his plate at supper tonight.

An older man pulled open the door and held it for a pretty woman. And there was our escape hatch.

Torrie got up and said, "May I help you?"

He clasped the woman's hand. "Yes, we'd like a room, one with an ocean view if possible. We're on our honeymoon."

The woman giggled, and I tapped Nikki's leg, gesturing to Milo while Monica and Torrie were distracted.

Finally, Nikki took the hint. "Well, this was so nice, but Lily, we need to get going. I have more baking to do today." She stood up and handed Monica the plate. "Keep the cake for you and Torrie to enjoy."

"Thank you. And stop by again if you think of more questions."

"We will." I opened the door for Nikki. "Thanks again, Monica."

Chapter 11
Lily

Once we got into the car with our seat belts buckled and Milo perched on Nikki's lap, I said, "What did you find out?"

"It took you long enough to come out to the car. I was beginning to think I should walk home." He looked at Nikki. "Wait until I tell Murphy how you made me wait and with important information too." He shook his head and made a *tsk-tsk* sound.

"Milo." I heard the exasperation, and he glared at me. "We were gathering information, and I bumped into Celeste Jaden too. We're going to need to get home and jot all of this down."

He cocked his head. "Lily, slow your jelly roll. I happen to know that all three suspects have left the motel, and it just so happens they seem to favor sunlight so the blinds are up on the windows in the back."

"We can't go snooping in windows in broad daylight." I glanced at Nikki, remembering the first time we had tried when we were attempting to clear Aunt Mimi's name during the investigation into Flora

Gray's murder. We almost got caught, and that was at dusk.

"You can't, but I can." He paused as if giving time for the dramatic music to swell like in a movie.

"Cut the suspense-filled moment and tell us what you saw."

Nikki scratched behind his ears, hoping it might relax him and help him get the words out. With Milo, you could never tell. As my impatience mounted, I turned the key and the engine purred to life. "We're going home, and on the way, you can fill us in. I don't want the magicians to come back and catch us in the act of loitering."

I backed around, and coming in the drive was Gage's police-issued sedan. He was behind the wheel, and Dax was in the passenger seat. Despite him knowing that we were coming out here, it felt like we'd been caught with our hand in the proverbial cookie jar. Should we stop to chat or just wave and drive away? Deciding it would be less awkward to chat now, I slid my window down as Gage pulled up next to us. He had done the same.

"Hello, ladies, Milo." He glanced into the empty back seat. "Fancy meeting you out here."

Under his breath, Milo said, "Detective, you're one step behind the puzzle master as usual."

Dax cracked a smile, so it was obvious that he heard my familiar's one-liner. Gage narrowed his eyes and looked at Milo. "Are you giving me a compliment, or that snark I think you're famous for?"

Milo half closed his eyes and focused his attention on licking his paw and proceeded to clean his face.

"He was just saying it's nice to see you here." I gave Dax a sharp glance, hoping he wouldn't spill the beans and tell Gage what my familiar had really said.

"It's nice to see him too. But why is he with you? Typically, you don't take him when you're poking around."

I squirmed in the driver's seat. "What makes you think I'm questioning people and not just visiting with the ladies?"

"Do you often stop by the motel to have coffee with Monica?" A knowing smile tugged the corners of his mouth. "Fess up, Lily. You and Nikki are out here questioning Monica about the magicians."

"Yes, but I didn't knock on their doors so I didn't break a promise."

Giving me a stern smile, he said, "Well, that is a nice change of pace, and promise me you won't."

I vacillated between just saying the words and thinking how I could rephrase them so it would make us both happy. Between the four humans and one familiar, we all knew I tended to do whatever needed to be done to solve a puzzle. Even if that meant knocking on a door and getting invited into a dangerous situation.

"In my defense, I never intentionally put myself in the danger zone. It just kind of happens." I lifted my shoulder to support my claim of innocence. Gage was looking at me, and despite wanting to drop the car into drive and leave, I was sure there was something they knew that might help me. "Have you discovered anything useful?"

Dax didn't look at Gage. Instead, his laser-like focus was on me. "Nothing that you won't find out if you stop by the theatre and chat with Mr. Schwartz. We might as well tell you."

I could feel my grin forming. "Go ahead, I'm all ears."

"He hadn't booked a show with the group. They showed up a few days ago and announced they were going to perform a single show."

"That's audacious."

He nodded. "The lack of respect for events at the Lights Out is annoying, but at least it's not upsetting to Alfred as he claims they would take care of filling the room with paying customers. And for him, I'm sure he saw dollar signs for admission and then again for concessions."

"Wouldn't he have to pay them some part of that?" Nikki asked.

"Compensation wasn't discussed." Gage glanced at Dax. "But Nikki brings up a good point. When we have a follow-up conversation with Alfred, that will be one of our first questions."

"I'll ask him when we stop in once we get to town."

"Lily," Gage said sharply. "Stay away from the theatre, and just go home. We don't have any idea what we're dealing with, and who knows, you might be the next target."

I huffed out a breath. "Doubtful since they need to pin this murder on someone and currently, I'm their scapegoat."

Milo tapped my hand with his paw, his claws barely pricking my skin. I looked down at him. "What?"

"We should leave and let the police do their job." He gave me a pointed kitty look. "Now, please."

"We will." I turned away from him, and this time he scratched my hand a little harder.

"We need to leave. Now."

There was a tone in his gravelly voice I had never heard before. Something inside of me pinged; the nerves in my stomach that were usually dormant sprang to life.

"Are you clairvoyant or something?"

But Milo didn't answer me. He only stared into my eyes.

"Gage, we can talk later. I'm going home, and that's where I'll be for the rest of the day."

Milo gave a brief nod of his kitty head and then lay down on Nikki's lap, settling in for a little snooze.

He looked so relaxed I thought of changing my mind and going to see Alfred and maybe cruise by my shop, but that jangling on my insides had me staying the course. "Call me later or better yet, why don't we all have dinner together."

Dax said, "I'm free."

Nikki chimed in, "I'll make dessert and Steve will be happy to see everyone."

"Good, it's settled. Dinner's at six." I slid the window up and drove out of the parking lot. Milo exhaled and placed his head on Nikki's knee. I guess leaving was the right thing to do, but would he tell me why? I wouldn't press him at the moment, but when we got home, it was time for a few questions, and he'd better be ready to give me answers.

After we arrived home and Milo had trotted through the kitty door ahead of us, Nikki put on the teakettle, and I adjusted the clue board so we both had an excellent view. There were notes that I needed to add, and Milo had to share what he had seen in the motel rooms. Especially if he could see into Luca's room—that could be illuminating.

Nikki moved about the kitchen, adding tea leaves from the stash my mom kept me supplied with. She didn't need to ask where anything was since we both knew the other's home as well as our own. I was wishing we hadn't left the cake with Monica and Torrie, but I really didn't need any more sweets, and Nikki had mentioned there would be dessert with dinner tonight.

I groaned, and she looked my way. "What's wrong?"

"Dinner. I have to cook or at the very least call for take-out." I slumped into the chair. "I wish part of my witchiness as a kitchen wiz would surface. This being an eclectic witch should have me being able to at least cook a decent meal if nothing else."

She chuckled. "Why do you need to be good at everything? Leave something to us lesser witches."

"What are you talking about? You're the best kitchen witch I know and what can I do other than dabble in different spells that come in handy when I get in a tough spot."

"Are you kidding. You've figured out how to control lights."

"Yeah, right. I caused a blackout. Some great feat there."

Nikki sat down next to me and grinned. "So, there've been a few bumps along the way. But you learned something I can't do, and you know a lot of spells that I've never even seen before. With Aunt Mimi guiding you, and Milo as your familiar, great things are in store for your future." She placed a hand over her heart. "As a Michaels witch, your powers are very strong, and despite that you got a late start, you're much better at everything even after these few short months than I was after two years."

I wished I could believe her, but she was my best friend. Of course she would say nice things to lift me out of the doldrums. "If I'm so fantastic, how could I have let down my guard so that someone could enter my house and steal my necklace? Do you realize what might have happened? My book was in the house. They could have taken it, but for some reason they must not have searched for it and thought I would leave it at the shop."

Nikki cocked her head and narrowed her eyes. "Maybe they didn't want to take the book. Could it be the most important thing to whoever broke in was to take the key and necklace to frame you for Luca's murder? He was the only one who seemed keen on discovering it and wanting it for his own. Or did you get the vibe they were all interested?"

I thought back to what had happened only two days ago, which in this moment felt like a lifetime. "Iris was excited when she saw it on the counter, but I got the impression it was more that Luca wanted it and she was just happy she could help him procure it."

She slapped the tabletop. "Exactly. He was the one all about the book. So one of those three wanted Luca dead."

"Why not all three? They could have been working together. Maybe, due to their age differences, Clay, Iris, and Celeste wanted to take the magic act in a new, fresh direction and he was keeping them under his thumb."

"Lack of professional opportunities could make a person mad. But mad enough to kill someone?" She chewed on her bottom lip.

I said, "The reasons for murder are love, money, or revenge. With three performers instead of four, there is a bigger cut of the profits. Maybe one of them had a romantic interest in Luca and jealousy was the motive, or could Luca have done something to one or all three and revenge was the reward?"

"That will be difficult to prove. Unless Celeste said something that lends itself in that direction."

I got up and selected a piece of yellow chalk so it would highlight the new notes from the first ones. Calling over my shoulder for Milo to join us, the teakettle whistled, and I was surprised Nikki had made tea the non-magical way.

She laughed. "Sometimes it's good to stay grounded by going old-school."

With a flick of my wrist, I turned the burner off. "And

in my book, I need all the practice I can get with being magical."

Nikki stood up. "That's why together we make the perfect witch, complimenting each other's strengths."

As she fixed the tea, that made me wonder. Tapping the chalk to my lip, I wrote down 1?, 2?, 3? And then in the next column I listed Clay, Celeste, and Iris. Right now, I wasn't sure how many murderers were involved, but even with Luca Rand coveting my family's book of magic, he deserved justice. I was determined to help Gage and Dax find it.

Milo strolled into the room and hopped up on a chair. "I take it you're finally ready to work this case?"

I glanced over my shoulder. "We're not the police, so we call it a puzzle."

"Excuse me, Ms. Witch."

I laughed at his kitty grumbles. "Milo, why don't you tell us what you discovered first, and then I'll write down the highlights of my conversation with Celeste."

He seemed pleased with this idea. "For starters, there was a black book that looks a great deal like your copy of *Practical Beginnings* in Luca Rand's room, and I'd bet my helping of smoked salmon that he planned to substitute a phony spell book for the real one and then hustle out of town."

"Why do you say it was Luca's room?"

"It was the only room where the bed hadn't been slept in which is logical since it wasn't announced he had died until well after housekeeping would have tidied the motel room. The other three are slobs. Clothes everywhere. Just disgraceful that people would make such a mess in the course of a few days."

"From my conversation with Celeste, they've been here

almost a week." I jotted down the information about the other black book, making a note on the board to ask Gage about it.

Milo said, "You'd better change that to Dax. Just in case it's a magical book and not a phony copy, he'd know the moment he touched it."

I added Dax to that same note. "What else did you see from prowling around?" I could feel my face squish up. "How did you see in the rooms?"

"I'm a cat, right, so I can walk on a windowsill, jump down and back up. Easy as getting a fish off a hook for me." Milo hopped down and stalked across the room, wrapping himself around Nikki's legs, hoping she'd give him a treat.

Under my breath so they couldn't hear me, I said, "That's almost as easy as me unlocking a door. I'd like to touch and see that book for myself."

Chapter 12
Gage

When Dax and I arrived at Lily's, it was five minutes till six. The smell of fresh baked bread teased my taste buds, and I couldn't wait to see what else was in store for dinner. Taking the back steps at a rapid pace, I said, "I hope you're hungry."

He patted his stomach. "Starving. Lunch was hours ago, and after going over every square inch of the bookstore again, I've worked up an ogre-sized appetite."

My hand was on the doorknob when I looked his way. "Have you ever met one to know they are extraordinarily hungry?"

"Yes, haven't you? Living in Pembroke Cove, there are plenty of magical communities nearby."

"Not that I'm aware of. It's just witches and maybe a mermaid or fairy. But nothing else."

He shrugged one shoulder. "You know Nikki mentioned other beings could come into town during the spring. Well, it's April and that means anything is possible."

"Not on my watch. Besides, I have my hands full with the non-magicals and witches in town. I don't want to face the unknown anytime soon." The door pulled away from me, and I stumbled to regain my balance. Lily was standing in the doorway, her smattering of freckles complimenting her sable-brown eyes. She looked like a fairy with her chestnut-colored short pixie cut hair, and I loved there was a smidge of flour on her cheek. Had she been baking without magic? I had to wonder how edible dinner was going to be.

"Hey, guys. I wondered if you'd be on time or if there would be some big breakthrough in the case that might keep you from the supper table." She pulled the door open wide and stepped aside so that we could come inside.

I brushed my lips over her cheek, and they grew pink. "How was the rest of your day?"

"Busy." She waved a hand in the direction of her clue board which was in its customary spot next to the table, set with five dinner plates and cutlery.

"What time is Steve coming over?"

"Oh, he's already here. He's just washing up in the restroom and will be out momentarily," Nikki said. The mention of Steve's name added a telltale twinkle in her eyes, and I was happy to see the honeymoon year had begun.

Rubbing my hands together, I crossed to the stove. "What are we having?" I picked up the lid on the cast iron pot, and my mouth began to water as the savory smells curled up from the bubbling gravy.

"Nikki gave me a cooking lesson that comprised of some non-magical tasks along with a few spells to help things along, and we made French sourdough bread, beef stew, and for dessert a berry crumble."

"That sounds like it will hit the spot." I lifted my eyes to Nikki, and she giggled before she said, "I promise it is all delicious, and Lily really did make everything."

Tapping her slippered foot on the polished wooden

floor, I could hear the mild annoyance in her voice as Lily said, "Gage, you're acting like I'm about to poison you or something even worse."

"Not at all. I'm just surprised since you always defer the baking to Nikki." I slipped my arm around her shoulders and gave her a one-armed hug. "And Dax and I are starving, so hopefully you've made plenty for us all."

"If not, you can fill up on bread. There are two loaves fresh from the oven." She gestured for us to take a seat. "The sooner we finish dinner, the quicker we can share what we know about the case."

Dax glanced my way and pulled out the chair closest to him. By the look on his face, he didn't want to talk about the case, even though we both knew that was the impetus behind the invitation to dinner.

Steve walked in as I was trying to formulate my response. I extended my hand, and his clasped it, giving me a firm handshake. "Gage. I heard you and Dax were coming to dinner tonight. Good to see you."

"Welcome back. Did you have a good time away?"

He looked at Nikki, and the smile on his face said more than words could. "It was great." Steve then shook Dax's hand. "Good to see you."

"Thanks." He grinned. "The ladies seem to have outdone themselves with dinner."

"My wife is an excellent cook."

Steve's smile grew even wider if possible, and for a moment, I wanted to wear a smile just like his. Lily and I got engaged last fall. She wanted to enjoy this time in our lives since we had gone from being best friends to a short romance and then to engaged. She had come close to catastrophe three times in the last several months, and I finally figured out that life wasn't a guarantee, so when she said yes to my proposal, I was over the moon with her.

Dinner was amazing, and Lily's culinary skills had improved. It had been a long running joke with our friends and family that she didn't enjoy cooking but could feed people, so I was usually the one in front of the stove. "Lily, dinner was delicious."

She beamed. "I'm impressed myself. Who knew I could make a stew that would make me sorry to see the bottom of the pot."

Nikki laughed. "I've come to realize you can cook."

"It's just not my thing. Besides, Gage and I agree he's going to be the primary chef when we get married."

"At least I'll have something to contribute, being non-magical. I actually learned by slicing fingers open and scrubbing pots after I burned food."

Everyone laughed, and I really enjoyed evenings like this, with good friends sitting together after sharing a meal. The only shadow hanging over us was the murder in Lily's shop and the other little detail that she was the prime suspect to anyone outside of this room.

Steve and I got up and cleared the table. It was time to get down to the task at hand, comparing notes about the murder of Luca Rand.

Lily moved the clue board so everyone had a clear view and Milo slunk into the room and made a complete circle before jumping into Dax's lap. Milo meowed, and Dax scratched his ears. The green-eyed monster stabbed my heart. Milo never went to me that easily. But Dax was a witch, and he could communicate with Milo, so I guess it was understandable. Maybe Milo would use Dax to convey vital information about this case. I had only been able to understand what Milo was trying to tell me once when Lily was being held captive in this very kitchen before Christmas. I shuddered just remembering that she had been coerced into drinking a drug that would erase her memory.

Lily caught my eye and raised a brow. I pointed to the coffee pot, and she shook her head. I wasn't in the mood for coffee either, but I still offered to make some.

Nikki said, "Take a seat, Gage. We're fine for now."

When all eyes turned to Lily, she said, "The case is lacking information, but today when Nikki, Milo, and I went out to the motel, I caught a break and bumped into Celeste Jaden." Milo meowed, and she said, "Hold your hairballs. We'll get to your information in a few minutes."

Dax continued to rub his ears, and Milo seemed to settle in and purred.

"As I was saying, Celeste was a little hostile, but she did tell me that the four of them met in magician school on the West Coast, and yes, it is a thing. Luca was a teacher, and they struck up a friendship. My guess is Clay, Iris, and Celeste were the most talented students, and Luca more or less recruited them. I'm guessing his need to be a stronger magician was enhanced with their skills."

"What exactly can they do?" I asked.

"Celeste didn't say if they had any special talent, but they've been honing their act for the last few years as they've worked their way east. Luca was determined to get back to Pembroke Cove and get his hands on my book. It was pretty obvious that was his motivation and under the guise of a traveling show, made it less targeted." She shrugged. "I'm not sure if that's the best way to describe it. but it's how I feel. I believe Aunt Mimi and the bookstore have been on his mind ever since he tried once to get the book from her and was unsuccessful."

"When Peabody and Mac spoke with Alfred Schwartz, he hadn't booked the magicians for a show, but they convinced him it was a great idea and they almost guaranteed a packed house. I find that very interesting."

Lily nodded and made a note on the board. *No show. Booked after arrival.* "And Torrie said they checked in almost a week ago, which is sooner than I thought, based on that first conversation in the bookstore. I was under the impression they had just arrived in town and came to the shop. But knowing Alfred's information, they had time to convince him of the show to make their visit legitimate for when they came to see Mimi."

"It's clear that Luca was running the operation," Dax said. "He was the person who wanted to come to town. I'm sure the other three had never heard of or wanted to even know Pembroke Cove existed, let alone visit. It's cold and damp and not a hot spot for tourists this time of year."

I snorted. "Some locals aren't even a fan of early April."

A smile tweaked the corners of Lily's mouth, but she quickly returned to her sleuth mode. "Celeste also said that Iris seems to have assumed control over the show which gave me the impression that was going over like a lead balloon."

I nodded, understanding how that could breed resentment which could escalate, at the very least, to an argument. People did kill for less reasons than a pecking order in a show. Especially one that could make a lot of money.

Milo bobbed his head and meowed at Lily.

"Alright. I'll tell everyone now."

He made what sounded like a grumble of satisfaction and relaxed again with Dax. "Milo, do you want to come sit with me?" I had to try. At some point in the not-too-distant future, we would be living under the same roof.

He meowed, and Dax smirked.

"What did he say?"

Dax said, "I'll tell you later." And then he winked at Lily which caused her to chuckle.

"While Nikki and I were having coffee with Monica and Torrie, our four-legged sleuth went on his own mission. It seems being a cat has its advantages. Like he can walk on narrow ledges and scope out rooms if the curtains are open."

I sat up straighter in my chair. We hadn't searched the three friends' rooms, but we had looked in Luca's and there wasn't much to find. "If Milo found something that can clear you, his next round of smoked salmon is on me."

Lily tapped the chalkboard, drawing our attention to the words *big black book – Gage? Dax?* "Milo was able to see into Luca's room, and I'm sure this is in the report, but Dax, you need to go back to the motel tomorrow and check this book out. Milo believes this was a substitute for my book, and we all think it might have been spelled to lead me to think that it was mine. And since you're the only one with access and magic, it has to be you."

I could feel the frown appear on my face, and I knew it was because I had to rely on someone else other than my skills for certain parts of this crime. Anxious to change the subject to something where I felt like I was actively involved, I said, "Do you want to know what else we learned today? We discovered a few clues at the bookstore."

Lily nodded as her eyes grew wide, and with a flicker of interest, she homed in on me. "Like what?"

"One, the bolts were loosened magically, at least that's what Dax discovered since they were unscrewed from the wall and they looked brand new. The time of death was in the early morning hours, and he was drunk. His blood alcohol was off the charts."

She jotted down the information about the bolts, time of death, and the fact Luca was inebriated, but it didn't make sense. Tapping the chalk on her chin, she murmured, "Why would he have been drinking so heavily that early in the morning? It doesn't make any sense."

I continued. "True, but maybe Luca and the others were celebrating the night before the book was found, and in their mind, the quest was almost over, especially if the book that Milo saw in his hotel room was intended to replace your book. Sounds like it might have been close to being the perfect switcheroo."

There was more to what happened at her store, and none of this was adding up.

She asked, "Dax, if the bolts were in good shape, how can you be sure they were the actual bolts from the wall?" She was studying her clue board as if magically a video reenactment of the events would appear. If only it were that easy.

He was rubbing Milo's ear, and her familiar was kneading his front paws into Dax's leg. Based on the contented look on Milo's face, there was no place he'd rather be. *Traitor*, I thought, but I'd find a way to win him over, even if I had to buy stock in smoked salmon.

Dax paused for several long moments as if he was summarizing his thoughts. "Someone could have encouraged Luca to look around for the book, climbed on the stool, and quickly performed a spell to loosen them. If he had been drinking, as it seems, it would have been easy to get him to stand in place while the perp pushed the bookcase over, then took off, leaving him to be discovered by you."

She popped a hand on her hip and half closed her eyes,

picturing the scene in her head. "I typically go to the shop around nine to get ready for the day. If they had broken in before sunup, surely someone must have seen something. Fishermen are headed to the marina."

"That's a good point, and it's something we'll check out tomorrow," I said. "Oh, and before I forget, you should think about replacing the stool. When Dax was getting down from examining the bolts, it listed to one side and was very unsteady."

The look of aha burst onto her face. Lily said, "There it was, the one thing that had been niggling at me since we started talking about the murder. Gage, what stool are you referring to? I have a stepladder that I use in the shop, so it folds flat when not in use."

That's when the lead landed in the pit of my stomach. "Well, that's not good."

Lily shook her head, dismay filling her eyes. "We need to get to the shop bright and early and check it out."

Chapter 13
Lily

Early the next morning, I was standing on the sidewalk in front of my store, waiting for Gage and Dax. Last night they had told me the shop had been secured magically with a spell. I wasn't as worried we'd find any surprises inside, but this mysterious stool had me perplexed. I needed to see it with my own eyes. I had shot a text to Aunt Mimi to see if she had left a stool in the storeroom, but she said no, just the small ladder I was using. It didn't take a genius to figure out someone brought the step stool to the store, but the bigger question was, why?

Gage and Dax were striding down the sidewalk, their long legs making the distance between us evaporate. They were such a contrast. They were both tall, whereas Gage had light-brown hair and eyes and he was well toned. Dax was thin, with dark hair and dark almost black eyes and was always wearing pressed jeans and a dark shirt and jacket despite that I had taken him shopping for more casual clothes better suited for small-town life. I had toyed with the idea of dating Dax for a hot minute, but we both quickly figured out we were better off as good friends, and of course that happened when Gage and I were stuck in the friend zone.

Gage's eyes locked on mine, causing my heartbeat to quicken, and his smile grew wider the closer he got. Oh, how I loved this man. "Good morning, gentlemen." I lifted my face to get a kiss from my fiancé.

"Hello, Lily. You look like you slept well last night." Dax gave me an approving nod. "That little something I gave you in your tea helped?"

"It did, and thank you for offering. I didn't think I would get such a deep sleep with all that's going on." I took Gage's hand and squeezed. "Today I can approach our little problem with a clear mind and fresh eyes."

He narrowed his gaze. "You're going to let us do our job, aren't you?"

I gave an impish smile and a small shoulder shrug. "I wouldn't say that I'm here just to observe. I know the place better than anyone, and that includes Aunt Mimi. After all, I've been running the shop for the last several years and some things have changed."

Dax smiled. "She's got us there. We'd never know if something was out of place or didn't belong here." He moved to unlock the door, and I noticed he only pretended to use a key. I was so impressed with his skill level and hoped that someday I'd be as good.

Dax entered first, and we waited on the sidewalk. It was best for him to make sure there wasn't anyone or any lingering magic that would be overshadowed by Gage and me being inside, almost as if just the act of walking into the space would disperse the air.

He disappeared from my sight and within moments was back. "Come on in, all's clear."

I covered my mouth, and a small moan escaped my lips

when the mess was staring me in the face again. Today I realized the side of the wooden bookcase was cracked, which must have happened during the fall. Books were everywhere and not just from this shelf but the next row over as well. In addition, there was a fine white dust everywhere.

"Gage, I'm assuming the white dust is from taking fingerprints, but how come it's white?"

He steered me to a wingback chair and gently eased me into the chair. I flashed him my best annoyed look.

"Lily, I don't want you accidentally touching anything. This is still a crime scene, and in all honesty, I shouldn't have brought you but discussed the situation with you at the station."

He held up his hands as I opened my mouth to protest why sitting me on the sidelines was illogical. "However, the circumstances are unusual, and with magic involved, this is the best course of action. For the moment, can you sit in the chair and let us take another look around before you start assessing the scene?"

In all of his long explanation, I could see there was some kind of sense to it. But he hadn't answered the question about the fingerprint dust residue. "Fine, I'll stay here if you tell me why Peabody and Mac used white dust. Does it do anything special?"

He chuckled. "Leave it to you to question our methods, but black dust is used on lighter-colored objects. With the bookcase being black walnut along with many other pieces of furniture in the store, it's best to use white so we don't miss anything."

With a touch of snark in my voice, I said, "That was a good idea. Sharon must have thought of it." Since I was relegated to a chair while they investigated, I switched to the other wingback which had a better view of the entire store. When Gage wasn't looking, I did a little spell to adjust the chair without making a sound, and now I had an unobstructed view. When he looked over his shoulder at me, probably to confirm I was following his orders, I gave him a sweet smile as the flicker of confusion furrowed his brow. Did he realize I was four inches to the right? "I hope it's okay I moved to this chair. I can armchair sleuth, while of course complying with your request that I stay out of the way."

"That's fine." He turned his attention back to the stack of books in front of him and withdrew a pair of latex gloves from his jacket pocket and pulled them on.

I noticed Dax had done the same when he leveled his gaze on me. A slight smile tugged at his lips. Each witch's magic seemed to have a signature that other witches could pick up on, and he knew what I had done. The only question was if he'd spill the beans to Gage. He shook a finger in my direction like my grandma did when she scolded me when I was five years old. I had to smother a laugh so as not to expose the truth to Gage.

It wasn't like I wanted to sneak around. I would tell him later, but right now, I needed to see what was going on and clear my name. If the situation didn't improve, I might be in more serious trouble than any of us could get me out of.

With Dax refocused on the bookcase and the outline where Luca had been found, Gage walked around the other side of the toppled bookcase, picking his way over more fallen books. I held my breath, hoping he wouldn't walk on them. The way he was stepping around them caused me to notice they were shaped like an S. That had to be deliberate. My witchy sense tingled. Could that be a clue? I wanted to get up and see for myself but not wanting to upset Gage, I said, "Would you take pictures of the book titles starting closest to me and moving back to the wall where that stool is, and take pictures of all sides of the stool too?"

He tipped his head and pointed to the books at his feet. "These?"

I nodded. "Yes. From this vantage point, the way they're placed looks like a capital S, and I have a hunch it might be a clue. I'd like to see the title of each book."

He leaned in close and took a picture of each cover in sequence, moving from the front to the back wall. I leaned to the left and watched as he finished taking pictures of the stool. Then he stepped over the row of books and crossed the room to my desk, picking up a pad and pen.

Handing me the paper, he said, "I'm going to text these images to you, but I don't see anything out of the ordinary other than they're neatly arranged and all mystery books."

My cell started to ping with incoming messages, and I didn't need to look at it to know they were the pictures. "How many books in total are there?"

"Has to be over twenty. Do you think the titles could mean something about the case?" Gage kept sending me texts and finally said, "The last four are of the stool."

He was waiting for my answer as I scanned the images. "I'm hopeful, but at first glance, they're just random Agatha Christie books. Whoever put them there meant to be annoying and nothing more." My phone vibrated twice with more incoming texts. One was from Nikki and the other from Aunt Mimi.

"If you need something else, let me know. I'd say in about fifteen minutes you can check things out for yourself."

"Good." I held up my phone. "I'm going to check in with Nikki and my aunt before I get started."

Dax called to him, "Gage, come take a look at this."

While they lifted a stack of books, I turned my attention to my text messages. Aunt Mimi had asked how everything was going and said that she had been sorting through some old papers from the time she and Luca had dated briefly but hadn't come across anything of relevance. I shot a quick thank-you text and said I'd call later.

I then read Nikki's message. *Hi, let me know what time we're meeting at your place to go over the new clues. I'll bring lunch or whatever.* She was the best friend I could ever have. I shot her a reply, saying I'd let her know. Setting my phone aside, I thought about the twenty-plus books. I drew what looked like the ribbon of books on the floor with space to write in each square that represented a book. The next step was to write down the titles and see if I could come up with a logical pattern that would indicate what it meant. Considering this was a deliberate placement, I felt it was critical to the investigation even if Gage and Dax had dismissed it.

I picked up my phone and scrolled through the images. As I thought, each book was an Agatha Christie title. Taking a closer look, some of these titles were not books I stocked in the store. Whoever did this brought the books with them.

"Gage. Do you want to see something strange?"

He and Dax stopped whatever it was they were doing and walked over to see what I was studying.

"Lily, those are the pictures I just took."

I rolled my eyes. "Obviously. But some of these books are old and not titles I carry in the store."

He gave me a blank stare before saying, "Are you sure?"

"I think I know my own inventory, but do you know what this means?" Before either of them could answer, I said, "The books were brought into the store to leave a message. Someone is trying to tell us—well, maybe me— about what happened or maybe even why."

Dax leaned in closer. "Or they're taunting you with a message."

I hadn't thought of that. I was leaning toward the opposite idea, but he was probably spot-on. "In either case, I'm going to figure out what it is." I nodded to the room. "Can I get up and look around if I promise to keep my hands in my jeans pockets?"

Dax said, "Yes. And there is something I'd like to show you first." He didn't look at Gage but waited for me to get up and pointed me to the back room. "In there."

Finally, I was getting into the action, and I was more than ready. I would work on the book titles when I got home with Nikki, and maybe even Milo could help. He had a gift for funneling down information in a way I often overlooked. "Lead the way."

Gage said, "Remember, looking only."

I could hear the overprotective tone in his voice, and I knew he'd prefer I was at home out of what he perceived as harm's way. But if I wasn't in the shop, I'd be cruising around town looking for answers. And if I wanted to point that out, it might just push him over the edge today. The one thing that did give me pause was, could someone be watching us from across the town green? I glanced in that direction but didn't see anyone; however, with all the trees and shrubs, there were places that provided good camouflage.

I flashed him a sweet smile. "Hand me a pair of gloves, just in case."

"Lily."

Now his intention was clear, I wasn't getting gloves. My smile grew wider, and I said, "Can't blame a girl for trying."

Dax cleared his throat as if breaking the tension between us, even if it was all one-sided and not mine. I followed him into the back room and stopped in the middle.

"I want to walk you through what I think happened, and if you could keep your eyes open and see anything out of place or just plain wrong, like you did with the books, let me know."

Looking around, nothing seemed out of place. I opened the cabinets too. "Everything is where it should be. Maybe I should have installed a camera at the door. At least it would have been on film if someone entered through the back door."

Gage hovered in the doorway with a scowl on his face until a banging on the door had him rushing to the front. I hurried after him, and Dax was bringing up the rear.

When we got to the windows, sitting on the sidewalk was a birdcage and there were four doves inside. Gage opened the door, and I stepped outside. I looked up and down the street, but no one was in the vicinity, which further cemented my belief that someone or more than one person was in the park keeping an eye on me. I bent over to see if there was a note attached to the cage.

"Who do you think left the birds here?" Dax asked as he moved in front of me. Gage was on my other side. My bodyguards.

I bent to untie the envelope from the top of the cage when Gage handed me a pair of gloves. "Here, put these on."

I slipped them on. The back of the envelope wasn't sealed so the card inside slipped out easily. I read it out loud. "*Dear Lily, A token of gratitude. Sincerely, The Magi-*

cian." I looked from Dax to Gage. "What do you suppose they're grateful for?"

"A couple of possibilities spring to mind." Gage held out his gloved hand and examined the note. "One, someone is happy Luca Rand died in your shop. Two, maybe this was part of the plan after they successfully stole your family's book. Three, whoever killed Luca is thanking you for taking the fall."

A shiver raced down my spine as I scanned the park from one side to the other. By the time I looked at Gage and Dax, steel replaced the shiver. "I don't like being a pawn in someone's chess game. But they don't know who they're dealing with."

Chapter 14
Lily

As I pulled into my driveway, I didn't want to get out of the car. As long as I stayed in here, nothing else bad or weird could happen. Instead, I reflected on the events of the morning. I had gone back inside after Tucker had wandered across the street, seeing us standing on the sidewalk. He had graciously volunteered to take the birds. Then Dax and I looked around the back room, but nothing seemed out of place. In fact, if I hadn't known a tragedy had occurred out front, it would have been like any other day at the shop.

I rested my forehead on the steering wheel. My brain was whirling with everything that had happened, and now I needed to figure out what that ribbon of books meant. Was it a clue or just an artful arrangement to mess with my head?

A flash of gray landed with a thump on the hood of my car, and I wasn't alarmed as I peered through my fingers. Milo loved trying the surprise attack mode with me on a regular basis. So far, much to his dismay, it hadn't worked.

My solitary time at an end, I pushed open the door and grabbed my handbag.

He padded across the hood of the car and hopped down, falling into step beside me. "My dear witch, what are you doing out here?"

"Thinking." I unlocked the door and let Milo go ahead of me. "Nikki will be over in a little while. There's a new puzzle to solve, and I'll need both of you on this one."

I dropped my bag on the counter, crossed to the table, and opened my laptop. "Before she gets here, I need to print some pictures Gage took at the store. Someone deliberately placed a row of books on the floor in an S shape. It's a clue. I just don't know if it's to the killer's identity or something else."

"Someone took the time to pull books from the shelves and place them on the floor?" He crouched down and sprang to the table close to my computer.

"Not exactly. Some of the books didn't come from the store, so whoever it was had to bring them the night before or morning of the murder." I began to forward the images to my computer from the text messages and then snapped my fingers. "I need to turn the printer on." I hurried down the short hallway to my office, clicked it on, and checked the paper tray. Now I was ready.

A short time later, all the images were printed, one of each book cover, and I arranged them on the counters in the order from the floor. I pursed my lips as I contemplated each image.

"Might I suggest hanging them up. Also, add a number in one corner to keep the order straight in case you have to move them around. If you do, it will be easier not to lose track that way."

Nodding, I rubbed his ears. "Good idea."

The tape was in the junk drawer near the sink, and I added the sequential numbers to the lower right. Then I secured each image around the kitchen on the cabinets and walls. I even tacked a few on the refrigerator. While I did this, Milo silently observed. I could sense something was on his mind and if I waited for him to spill the beans, it might take a while. "Hey, why don't you tell me what's troubling you?"

He gave me an assessing look. "I don't like this."

His deep kitty growl surprised me. "What, that I'm hanging up the book covers?"

He cocked his head and gave me a look like I was off my rocker. Flicking his tail from side to side, annoyance came off him in waves.

I swept my arm around the room. "These?" I couldn't have Milo upset too. My gut had been rolling for days, not that I was about to verbalize that to anyone, including my familiar. "They're just clues like we've looked at before." I turned my back on him, not wanting my face or eyes to betray how I really felt. If I was being honest, his mini admission of fear shook me to my core.

"Lily." The way he said my name was as sharp as his claws. "This is very serious. The other times you followed clues and worked to solve a puzzle, it was never personal. Not like this. Someone is trying to set you up to take the fall, and I think in the process, they're going to attempt to take your book."

Whirling around, I said, "Luca wanted my book, *Practical Beginnings*, and he's dead so that idea is off base. But someone is doing their best to point the finger in my direction which is why it is critical to figure out this message." A knock on the back door derailed our conversation. I was expecting Nikki, but she would have tapped and then walked in.

I pulled the door open and was shocked to see Clay, Iris, and Celeste standing on my back deck. My first thought was why were they at my house, and the second was how had they found it. The polite thing to do was invite them inside, but the last thing I wanted was to be alone in my kitchen with three magicians of unknown magical power. Glancing over my shoulder at the papers covering my kitchen and then to Milo. He hopped down from the table and raced out the open door. That was the hint I needed.

"This is a surprise. Why don't we talk outside." It wasn't a question but a statement. The day had been overcast, but it had cleared, and despite the cool breeze, it was warm enough. I pulled the door closed tight, and in that moment, I wondered if I should send a quick summoning spell to Nikki. Instead, I wrapped myself and Milo in a protection spell as I silently thanked my little fur ball for drilling them into me until they were as easy as taking a breath.

I gestured to the small table and four chairs. "Please have a seat and you can tell me what's on your mind." And to myself, I thought, *this is about to get very interesting*. I patted my jeans pocket to record the conversation but I had left my phone next to my laptop on the kitchen table. I hadn't perfected moving objects yet so there wasn't much I could do at this point. Milo was perched on the porch railing to my right and my back was to the house. I had a clear line of sight to my three visitors as well as the driveway. "Can I offer you tea or coffee perhaps?"

Celeste glanced at her friends and then said, "This isn't a social call. We wanted to clear up a few," she cocked her head and said, "misunderstandings."

"I see." Not that I had any idea what she was talking

about except for the conversation we'd had outside the motel. Other than being a tad hostile, I couldn't attribute anything to her specifically.

Clay licked his lips and quickly looked between the two women before he trained his gaze on me. "I'll begin. Celeste mentioned that you had chatted, and she told you how we all met Luca from the magic school. I'm guessing you wondered how we could have gotten tied up with someone like him."

I cocked a brow, curious by what he meant, *someone like him*, but again this was their show, not mine, so I waited. It was a Gage tactic when he was interviewing a suspect or just wanted to get information. He wouldn't say a word and to fill the silence, people would just start talking and spill their guts. I had the distinct impression this was the only way to deal with these uninvited guests.

He continued. "Luca was charismatic and a great teacher. It was during one class that he casually mentioned he was looking for a few talented magicians to join him on a road tour. As the three of us became good friends, we started to talk about joining him, and we worked hard to perfect various tricks that he had said were important to master."

"It seems that you were very successful if you've been on the road for the last several years performing magic shows all over the country."

Iris piped up, "And Canada too. It has been a dream come true."

Her eyes got a faraway look, and I believed she meant that comment. "This is all very nice, but what brought you to my house today? Are you anxious to get back on the road and think I have some sway over Detective Peters?"

They looked at each other, brows furrowed. Celeste said, "I thought Detective Erickson was on the case."

"Normally, he is but..." I held up my left hand and wiggled my finger, knowing the sun would catch the stone and cause it to dance to its best advantage. "We're engaged, so it's a conflict of interest for him to be in charge. He handed the case over to Detective Peters."

"Oh, that we didn't know," Iris said. "Congratulations."

That had to have been the most insincere comment I'd heard yet, but again, I just kept waiting to learn more about their real motivation for coming over.

Clay got up. "Since Lily can't speak to the detective on our behalf, we might as well leave."

I felt my mouth gape open, and I shut it just as quickly. "What would I say to him for you?" Dang, these next few comments were going to be doozies.

"That you know we had nothing to do with Luca's death. It was an accident in your shop so in a way your negligence killed him." Clay put his hands on the table and leaned closer to me. "Not that I'm blaming you per se, but you really should do a better job with the maintenance in your store. You never know what might fall over or what people might trip over."

That sounded like a threat, but Clay knew more than he was saying. "Really? What exactly are you referring to?" My temper began to rise, but I did my best to keep it on simmer.

Iris patted Clay's hand. "Sit down. We agreed we weren't going to visit with Lily and accuse her of killing Luca. Anyone could see that it was a tragic accident, and after all, he was in her shop in the middle of the night. If he had decided to go back and look for her book during normal business hours, he would probably still be alive." She gave me a pointed look. "More than likely she still wouldn't have sold him the old musty copy, but I guess it would have been possible."

I tried to keep a smile on my mouth, but through gritted teeth it was difficult, and I said, "The book isn't for sale."

Celeste gave me a sickly-sweet smile. "Would you mind if we took a look at the book? I'm curious what the big deal is. After we hit the road and really developed our act, all Luca could talk about was working our way across the country in hopes he could buy it, no matter what the cost."

I stood, and the sound of the wrought iron chair against the decking grated on my last frayed nerve. "I'm sorry, the book isn't for sale. It never was and never will be. I can't help you with the police department. Once they're finished with the investigation and if you've been cleared, you'll be free to leave Pembroke Cove."

Clay's brow arched, and a sneer graced his mouth. "Don't you mean when you've been cleared? How could you even think his dearest friends would do anything to harm him? Actually, he's the star of our little show."

It was my turn to feign surprise. "Really, well, maybe with Luca out of the way, one of you can step up and become the new star."

An unmistakable, lustful gleam entered each person's eyes. They all wanted—no, craved—the center spotlight. Was this the motive for killing Luca Rand?

"How could we have been involved?" Celeste glanced at Iris and Clay. "What motive would we have? Whereas you have the real motive to strike him down. He tried to take the book from your aunt and he was back, this time more determined than ever to get his hands on it. Maybe he called you to arrange a meeting to discuss terms for a sale. After all, you couldn't tell your aunt you didn't have an interest in the book since you don't seem to have the same" —she looked from my eyes to my toes and back to my eyes again—"skills that she does. So, the book is of no use to you. And we also know from what Luca said that your little friend who barged in on us at the store is more like your aunt than you'll ever be. The four of us had a good laugh over it."

Clenching my fists at my sides, my magic began to cause my fingertips to tingle, but our motto was to do no harm. Not that I would lift my magic in anger, but I was ready if needed to defend myself even if right now all Celeste was doing was taunting me about things she knew nothing about. "What makes you think I'm not like my aunt?"

Iris smirked. "Everyone knows witches start their training long before now, and if you were a powerful witch like Mimi, you'd be oozing power like water off a duck's back."

I couldn't help myself, nor was I inclined to stop. I lifted my hands palms up and chanted soft but clear so they could hear every word. "The table before me is weightless and, chainless, now hovers above the magicians three. For this I wish, so it shall be."

Their eyes grew wide, and Celeste jumped up from her chair as it tumbled over and crashed to the floor. She clasped Iris's hand who pushed Clay out of their way.

I kept my hands in the same position, suspending the table from the floor, waiting to see what they would do next. I hoped they'd leave. As they headed to the steps, to my surprise they paused and turned to look at me.

Celeste said, "I guess we have proof that you could move the bookcase and cause it to come crashing down on poor Luca." A white lace hankie appeared in her hand from seemingly nowhere, and she dabbed the corner of her eye.

"This will be interesting information for a certain detective, don't you think?"

Iris flicked her long auburn hair over her shoulder and gave me a sly wink. "Very interesting." She looped her hand through Clay's arm. "Care to swing by the police station on our way back to the motel? This might be just the information they need to let us leave town."

"Do you think anyone will believe you three over me?"

Clay led the way down the steps, and he turned to look back, his face frozen in a smug expression. "I guess you'll just have to wait and see."

I knew taunting them wasn't in my best interest, but the magic that surged through my blood was like an itch I had to scratch. I let the table settle back to the floor and Milo said, "Well, that was interesting." He got up and arched his back. "Do you think it's possible they did it together? For the record, my money is on the three of them."

I sank to my chair. "All I know for sure is one of them did it, and we will find out who."

Chapter 15
Gage

Lily had left the store, and hopefully, she would work on the puzzle of the books and discover if they were random or if there was a special meaning. At first and even second glance, it just seemed like someone was leaving a deliberate mess to annoy and possibly even confuse investigators. But no clue was too small to examine in depth.

"Dax, you said Lily didn't notice anything out of place in the back room, but the working theory is that's how Luca and the killer came inside."

He was standing on the stepladder from the back room, examining the bolt holes again, and snapped a few more pictures. "What are you thinking?" I asked.

He stepped down and handed me a camera as he looked me in the eye. "I think whoever came with Luca entered and exited through the back, and I also think there had to have been more than one person with him. There had to be someone keeping Luca on task looking for the book while the other loosened the bolts. Even using magic, the person would need to have been focused on the task and not get distracted."

I wish I understood how magic worked, like if I had been able to do it, but that gene wasn't passed down to me even though my mom's magic was powerful. Dad's non-magical abilities were stronger in the DNA pool. For as long as I could remember, I had wondered but never asked anyone. Would Dax explain to me how it felt?

"Does it take a lot of practice to develop that level of skill?"

He took a step in my direction, a perplexed frown on his face. "For a magician, I couldn't say. I was born a witch."

Nodding, I said, "Right, but Lily didn't get her magic until she was older and started to read her family's book. Is it the same with your family?"

His face held a contemplative look. "Magic is different for every coven and family, and it also depends on the parents. In Louisiana, where my family's roots run deep, it's common knowledge our town is made up not just of witches but a few vampires, fairies, and even a werewolf or two. From what I've discovered so far, Pembroke Cove is primarily witches and most of them come into their powers slowly. In our coven, we are baptized in a cauldron."

He laughed as my face morphed into a look of shock.

"Not a real bubbling cauldron, it's just an expression. But I can't remember a time when I didn't know exactly who and what I was. It's a tight-knit community and everyone knows each other's strengths and supports the other."

It sounded like our small town but most of the locals were generational which indicated to me that magical families had been here for centuries. "If everyone is so close, why did you leave?"

He crossed the room and peered out the window as if gathering his thoughts. Dax and I had never gotten this deep into his life until today, but I felt like now was the time to ask.

Slowly, he began to speak. "I love my family, but deep inside, I felt like I was being called to be someplace else. It was as hard to explain then as it is now." He glanced my way. "I'm not sure if you can understand what I mean since you've never moved away from your hometown."

I had never wanted to live anywhere else, even when Lily and I weren't as close as we are now, but some of our friends from high school left for college and never came back, so on some level, I understood.

"Taking the unconventional route, I went into law enforcement. I figured with my special talents, I could make a difference in the non-magical world. But I was isolated from all that I had known, and it wasn't until I came here that I started to feel like I was making a difference."

"You have, even if we don't count in the time you saved Lily during the Halloween event." A shiver raced down my spine again when I thought of her coming so close to being killed. I pushed it to one side. Circling back to my original question of developing strong magic, I asked, "Has your magic changed since you've been gone, from Louisiana, I mean?"

"No. It's steady, but you have to remember I learned spells from the time I could focus. Even before I could talk, there were simple things I could do."

He smiled at what I guessed was a fond memory.

"When I was a kid and wanted another cookie or a piece of candy, I could get anything with focus. My momma used to brag about the strength of my talent and at such an early age. Even though I was being a naughty little kid, she decided it helped strengthen my skills. But with a magician, it would take years of practice to loosen bolts quickly."

Nodding, I said, "What about if they worked together? Could two people be even stronger?"

"Sure, but the more people who know a secret, the better the chance it will get out. A murderer wouldn't want that to happen. One person can always toss the other to the wolves, or in our case, the law."

"I thought of that too." My gut churned. We were getting nowhere fast. "We need to talk to the three suspects again."

"First, let's see what Lily has to say about the book titles. We could swing by her place, bring lunch, and go over the clues again. Because we must be overlooking an important piece of evidence."

"What's that?"

"The timing. Someone had to break through Lily's protection spell, take her necklace, and do a cursory look for the book. Then get down to the bookstore, lure Luca in, loosen the bolts, plant the necklace, and push the bookcase over, then leave knowing he was already dead or would be soon."

I snapped my fingers. "Do you know what has been bugging me? The tox screen that said he was inebriated. What if that was a spell too? Is it even possible?"

"I'll call the coroner's office." Dax had his phone out. "Hello, this is Detective Peters." He paused before saying, "Would you do me a favor? Something isn't adding up, and I'd like for you to run the blood test again to confirm Mr. Rand had been intoxicated." Again, he paused and this time his lips thinned. "I'm not suggesting you made a mistake. I'm asking you to double-check and call me as soon as you get the results." He rubbed his hand over his chin. "Thank you."

Looking at me, he said, "Why do people have to get so defensive? Did you hear me say I thought there was a mistake made?" Before I could answer, he said, "No. He's human, and machines and tests are fallible. Double-checking never hurt anyone."

I couldn't help but let a grin slip out. "It's good to see the cool façade you usually wear slip just a bit."

Chuckling, he said, "Don't tell anyone. I like being thought of as the moody cop." He pulled up the collar on his dark jacket. "Goes with the overall appearance."

"One more thing. You said you've been looking for a place where you feel like you're making a difference. Have you discovered what you're looking for here?"

"I'm not sure. I like Pembroke Cove, but I still feel like someone is missing from my life, but I'm not in any rush to leave."

I hoped he'd stick around. Good friends who knew your secrets and kept them were hard to find. As much as I liked Peabody and Mac, I wasn't going to tell them about the witches that lived in Pembroke Cove. If I hadn't grown up with a witch for a mom, I'd have a hard time believing that story. "I'll take that for now, but do me a favor. If you ever get the urge to pack your bags, let me know."

With a brisk nod of his head, he said, "Now let's take one last walk through and determine if we can give Lily back her store. I'm sure she's at loose ends, and there is not enough activity on this case to keep her occupied. The next thing we know, she'll be out tracking down the killer by knocking on one door at a time."

"Isn't that the truth." Which made me wonder. "Let me check in with Peabody. I want to know if they've recanvassed the shop owners and also have them ask around if anyone has installed security cameras. I'd like to think they aren't necessary, but after this run of murders, I'm going to talk to Lily about installing some both inside and out of this shop."

Dax grinned. "Can I be around when you suggest it?"

Cocking my head and narrowing my eyes, I said, "Why?"

"Oh, my friend, you have so much to learn about dating a witch. Asking them to use a mortal tool like a camera is like kicking sand on their spell book. It's just not done. And I guarantee you, she'll never let her protection spell weaken around her house or shop again. It will be as safe as the gold stored in Fort Knox."

Shrugging my shoulders, I said, "Then maybe I'd better skip that conversation, but my officers can double-check, just to make sure." I had to chuckle to myself though. Doubting Lily's skills would have perturbed her, and I'd forget about installing cameras, for now.

"You're right about clearing the shop and getting Lily back to work. Too much idle time isn't good for anyone, and that definitely includes her." I sent her a quick text letting her know we were coming by around lunch, and we'd pick up sandwiches. Within less than a minute, I got a message saying bring enough for Nikki and Mimi; they were already at her place.

"Lily's support sleuths are on the case."

Dax gave me a quizzical look.

I said, "Nikki and Mimi are at her place, so we need enough food for everyone."

"I'm going to take another round of pictures starting at the back door and work my way around the shop. Once I upload them, I feel confident it's safe to tell Lily she can get back to work in the morning. This way I'll have time to review the images tonight, just in case."

He walked into the back room, and I know he probably didn't hear me say, "That will make her happy." And it would help to know she was in the store and not able to just hop in her car at a moment's notice and head back to the motel to question Iris, Celeste, or Clay. I didn't want her anywhere near them. Without knowing how strong their magic was, it wasn't a chance I wanted her to risk.

As I walked the perimeter of the yellow tape with my eyes glued to the floor, I noted a hair clip partially under a book, wondering how we had missed it earlier. I took a couple of pictures on my phone and withdrew gloves from my back pocket. Slipping them on, I took a couple more pictures as I pulled the accessory out from under the book. Holding it up to the light, there were two long strands of auburn hair. *Celeste Jaden, we can now place you at the scene of the crime.*

Calling over my shoulder, I yelled, "Dax. Take a look at this."

He came into the room still taking snaps before shooting a couple of the clip in my hand.

"Looks like Ms. Jaden was here during the accident."

"Aren't you jumping to a conclusion?" Dax took the clip in his gloved hand. He turned it over to look at the back side. "How can you be sure it's hers and wasn't dropped by another customer?"

"Gut instinct and maybe a little wishful thinking. I want to get the focus off Lily and onto our most likely, and real, suspects."

He snapped open a small zippered plastic bag and slipped the clip inside. "There's one way to find out for sure. We'll ask during our Q and A session."

"This might be our first real break. I mean, we know Lily is innocent, but in order to get the real killer behind bars, we need proof, and this is a step in the right direction."

Dax removed his gloves and clapped me on the shoulder. "It's only a matter of time, my friend. Patience."

Without looking at him, I asked, "If your fiancée was the main suspect in a crime, would you have the patience to methodically sift through clues or would you just want to get the focus off her and on someone else?"

"You know the answer to that, Gage, and in case you've forgotten, we all care about Lily."

That was a gut punch. And Dax was right. We all wanted to clear the case, and fast.

Chapter 16
Lily

Aunt Mimi, Nikki, and I were standing in the kitchen with Milo sitting on a chair in his most human imitation and Murphy, Nikki's dog, stretched out in front of the hallway entrance. I was tapping a pen on the blank legal pad in my hand. "Twenty-three Agatha Christie books with two being written under her pen name Mary Westmacott." I moved to the first picture which was the first book in the row. "The sequence has to be deliberate, but we need to figure out if it's the title that's important or the subject matter."

Nikki said, "Or was it the year it was published, and does it matter who the sleuths are?"

Aunt Mimi looked at each picture and shook her head. "There are Miss Marple, Tommy and Tuppance, as well as Poirot books so that's not the connection. And they span her entire career. It's the names of the books that are the key." Aunt Mimi began to read them aloud.

N or M

Evil Under the Sun

Murder at the Vicarage
Endless Night
Murder of Roger Ackroyd
Unfinished Portrait
Nemesis
Death on the Nile
Elephants can Remember
The Rose and the Yew Tree
Lord Edgeware Dies
Sleeping Murder
The Under Dog
Ordeal by Innocence
The Sittford Mystery
Appointment with Death
The Thirteen Problems
Hickory Dickery Dock
The Mousetrap
The ABC Murders
Hercule Poirot and The Greenshore Folly
They Do It With Mirrors
Cards on the Table

Nodding, I said, "You're correct, but let's look at the first word in each title." Reading the first few titles aloud, I said, "N, evil murder endless murder unfinished nemesis. That's not even a sentence."

"Or is it a cryptic message?" Nikki asked.

I sat down at the table and wrote down the first word in each book title several times. "No, it's not a cryptic message; it has to have a point. Whoever did this went to a lot of trouble."

Mimi made her way around the room, looking at one cover to the next. "What about just the first letters?" Glancing over her shoulder, she said, "Write this down?"

With pen poised over the paper, I said, "Ready."

"N, E, M, E, M, U, N, D, E, T, L, S, T, O, T, A, T, H, T, T, H, T, C." I studied the page and groaned. "Still nothing that makes sense." I held up the pad, but neither Nikki nor Mimi could see the letters from across the room.

Milo looked between the three of us, and he said, "Do you have any poster board in your office? You could write it out and hang it up." He stretched over the cushion on the chair and said, "Wake me when it's time for lunch."

As much as I wanted to reply with a snarky comment, it was an excellent idea. I stepped over Murphy as I moved quickly down the hall and into my office. Grabbing several oversized sheets and different-colored markers, I smiled, knowing there was no way this was going to be an easy puzzle. It was like solving a crossword puzzle without any clues, and it was going to be so much fun. I could barely contain my excitement as I stepped back over Murphy. Aunt Mimi and Nikki wouldn't see this as fun, and it had been a long time since I had to dive into something this complex.

Nikki took the poster board and began to tack up sheets under several photos so we could work on each letter or word. Rubbing my hands together and tempering my voice, I said, "Challenge accepted, my unknown nemesis."

As I put extra emphasis on the final word, Aunt Mimi said, "You're using book titles in your sentences now." She screwed up her face into a silly expression and gave Nikki a smile. "It's going to be a very long day."

She pointed at the counter which was now covered with bakery boxes, plastic-covered bowls, and trays. "Not a problem. I have enough food, sweet and savory, to keep us well fueled."

"Since the first letters didn't work, let's move to the first words and see if they make sense. But I feel that the first word starts with *N* as it's the first letter of the first title."

I wrote down *N* under the cover of the first book. "I'll use that as my consonant."

Nikki said, "Add an *E* next. It needs a vowel and if we look at the pictures, there is a space between the fifth and sixth books and again before the last five."

"Good observation, Nik. If we take that as information, there are three words in this puzzle." I wondered how I had overlooked that as I wrote down an *E* next to the *N*. Following that same train of thought, I plugged in the first letters of the next three words and stepped back. "*N, E, M, E, M*," I said in a clear voice. "That's not a real word." I tried a few more combinations of words with the next letters, leaving the *N* and *E* as a constant. I took several deep slow breaths as I worked through the letters of the words. After a half hour, nothing looked like it was going to come together, and much like a crossword, I wanted to hop around, but the first word of any puzzle always helped to serve as the foundation to solving it.

I snapped the cap back on the marker and tossed it to the kitchen table. "At this rate, it's going to take us days to solve the riddle."

Grabbing the teakettle and crossing to the sink, I began to fill it. I wanted something mundane to distract me. Oftentimes clearing my thoughts helped me to focus. What kind of a message would the killer need or want to leave me? Or had Luca set up the message before he died? Or maybe it didn't have anything to do with the murder, but was a good way to poke at me for wanting to steal my book of magic. I must trust my instincts on this one, and it was a clue from the killer. All I needed to do was focus my energies on discovering what it was. I half turned from the sink to look at the first set of five books. What if the titles are less about the order they're in and more about one word holding the key to the five-letter word which we were focused on? Leaning against the counter with teakettle in hand, I continued to study the words in each title. "*N, E, M, N, E A, N, E, T, N E, V…*" I put the kettle aside and looked at the fourth book title. "The word needs another vowel. N E V E, N E V I." I shook my head. "N E V E." With a quick glance at the fifth word, I said, "N E V E R. Never."

I looked from Nikki to Mimi and then Milo who opened one eye as I exclaimed, "The first word has to be *never*."

Nikki got up from the table and wrote down under the first five covers, in bold print, *NEVER*. "Well, that burned a few brain cells."

I pretended to wipe proverbial sweat from my brow. A tap on the kitchen door before it opened had Gage and Dax sauntering in. They were holding pizza boxes, and Gage's eyes widened as he looked at the poster board and pictures hanging around the room.

"What's going on here?" He dropped a featherlike kiss on my mouth, and I leaned in and kissed him more firmly.

My heart skipped a beat or two as he looked deeper into my eyes. "I see you've been busy."

I took the box from him and nodded in the direction of the first word. "It's slowly coming together, but this has taken us all morning."

With a twinkle in his eye, Gage glanced around the room and said, "One word? Where's the puzzle master?"

"Standing right in front of you, but without any clues,

it's like solving a word jumble or crossword without clues to guide us."

Dax set the box he had carried in on the counter and flipped back the lid. "So, are you saying our timing is impeccable since more brain power is needed?"

"Something like that." I gave him a light punch in the shoulder. "What has the police force been focused on this morning?"

"Getting ready to give you good news." He tugged a lock of my short hair like an older brother would do.

I patted the center of my chest and arched a brow. He had my full and undivided attention. "You've caught the killer and we don't need to solve the puzzle?"

The corners of his lips dropped a bit. "Sadly, not yet, but we're actively working on it; however, we're not much closer to a strong suspect than yesterday."

I noticed a secretive look pass between Dax and Gage, but that could wait. I needed to know what might be a positive. "You were saying something good had happened?"

"Right." Dax refocused on me. "I'm going to release your shop back to you tomorrow morning. I'd still like you to keep it closed for a day, but you can get in and set things to rights."

I threw my arms around him and hugged him tight. "Thank you, Dax. This is great news." I turned to hug Gage even tighter if that was possible. "Does this mean that I'm off the suspect list?"

He kissed my cheek and lowered his eyes to the floor. "I wish. But it means there is nothing more to be gained from the bookstore, so there's no reason to keep it under lockdown."

I stepped out of his arms, and my heart dropped in a rapid descent. "Oh, I was hoping..." My voice trailed off, and I wiped away a tear that had suddenly appeared. I wasn't going to cry in front of anyone. There was no sense in having anyone feel sorry for me in this situation. They believed in me, and that was all that mattered for now.

The air was thick with worry, tension, and a smidge of relief about the shop reopening. At least that was how I was feeling. Nikki handed out plates to each of us. Gage held out my chair, and I sat down. His fingertips grazed my shoulder, providing me comfort. The gesture gave me a jolt of courage. I sat up straighter. There was no sense wallowing in being a suspect. I had to figure out this clue, and then there was work to be done to track down who was guilty. One of the remaining magicians was responsible, or maybe they worked together and it was all three of them. Looking at Dax and Gage, it hit me hard that they weren't any closer to learning the truth, and I had spent so much time over the last few days waiting on the sidelines for something to happen. Other than chatting with Monica and Torrie and deliberately chasing down Celeste in the parking lot at the motel, I had done nothing proactive. And that was about to change. Playing it safe wasn't going to find Luca's killer or clear me. I wasn't going to tell Gage that I was about to flip the switch and do what I do best. Solve puzzles.

Rubbing my hands together, I said, "Let's have some lunch."

Milo took that moment to slink into the room and wind around my legs. "Did you say one of my favorite words?"

I scooped him up and nuzzled him before he batted at my cheek with a soft paw. "Yes, we're going to have lunch, so stick around." I set him on the floor.

Dax looked around the kitchen. "You should bring us

up to speed with the pictures and what your current working theory is."

Gage placed his hand over mine. "If there's anyone who can solve this riddle, it's you."

I sat up straighter in my chair. "Thank you for believing in me." I looked at my friends and aunt. "All of you."

Aunt Mimi smiled. "Let's move past this emotional stuff and eat. I don't know about the rest of you, but my brain needs pepperoni to keep going."

Tipping my head to one side, I couldn't help but laugh. "This is a first—pepperoni being used for brain food."

Over slices and iced tea, I filled Gage and Dax in on our working theory. "The bottom line is this will be the hardest puzzle of my life. It's clear to me that what we've deciphered so far is a message. They're not random words just strung together." I pointed to the images. "When you look at the ribbon as a whole, you can see the two separations in the books. This is a three-word jumble without the clues."

Nikki's head snapped up. "And who is it meant for?"

Without blinking, I said, "Me."

The room fell silent as everyone contemplated the weight of my words. Without looking at Gage or anyone in particular, I broke the silence. "And I'm done hovering in the shadows. You need me to solve this crime, not just this little puzzle. Be forewarned. I will be taking an active part in tracking down the killers."

Gage blinked, and he locked eyes with me. "Killers?"

"I'm pretty sure that one person couldn't have committed this crime alone. It took planning. Breaking into my house, loosening bolts, getting Luca drunk, pushing over the bookshelf, and then bringing in the extra books to leave the message. There are only so many hours in a night to get all that done and not get caught in the act, and they're magicians, not witches."

It didn't escape my notice that Dax and Gage looked at each other with dour expressions.

"What? Is there something you know that I don't?" Neither of them spoke. "Look, if you don't tell me, I'll find out anyway. You might as well just save me time."

Dax said, "I got a call from the coroner's office right before we got here. Something was bugging me about the toxicology report. Given that Luca's blood alcohol reading was high but when we searched his room we only found soft drinks, I asked for the test to be ran again. It was a false positive. There is no evidence that he even had one drink, let alone enough to make him potentially unaware of what might be happening around him."

I thumped my hand on the tabletop. "That fits perfectly with my hypothesis that more than one person was involved."

Gage reached for my hand, and as much as I would have liked the connection, I knew he was going to attempt to sway my decision to leave the investigating to him and Dax. "No, don't say it."

Concern filled his eyes. "It's not wrong for me to be worried about you. If you're correct, this just got even more dangerous than we thought."

My heart softened for a fraction of a second before determination set back in. "I love that you're worried about me, but I need to see this through. I have Nikki, Milo, and of course all of you to be there if I need help. But there is one thing these magicians have done, and that is to underestimate my powers as a witch." I winked at Aunt Mimi. "And not just any witch, but one from a very powerful line of witches. What I lack in actual skills, I will make up for in talent simmering in the background."

My aunt beamed with pride. "Lily, you're right. There is one thing about being a Michaels witch—we are a force to be reckoned with."

With a brisk nod of my head, I slowly looked around the table from Milo to Mimi to Nikki to Dax and then Gage. "So, who's all in?"

Chapter 17
Lily

Later that afternoon, after everyone had left, Milo and I were still sitting at the kitchen table, studying the pictures of Agatha Christie book covers. I dropped my head on the tabletop and groaned. "Milo, what am I overlooking? So far, all we have is the first word. Never. Never what?"

With a low grumble, he said, "You need a distraction. What do you think of practicing a new spell? Every time you open it, the book seems to know exactly what you do need or will need."

I lifted my face from the legal pad and pushed my bangs out of my eyes. "True, but this time I need a clear mind to figure out what this message is and there won't be a spell for that."

"But you might learn something useful for the days ahead. If you're going to do what you said and get out there, putting yourself in the line of danger, you're going to need more spells flying out of your wand than ever before. Food for thought, whoever cast the spells over Luca is very powerful. I was speaking with Phoenix before breakfast, and she remembers the magician formerly known as Luca."

I sat up straighter. Talking with Aunt Mimi's familiar had been a stroke of genius, and I wish I had thought of it first, but it didn't matter. Milo always had my back. "And what did she say?"

Milo's eyes closed to a slit, pleased that I was finally coming around to quizzing him on what he knew. "Phoenix remembers the magician from years ago when he was semi dating Mimi. And I must say she didn't think much of him. To use her words exactly, 'he was a cad.'"

"A what?" I contained the laugh that threatened to bubble up. Why on earth was a familiar using such an old-fashioned word?

He swished his tail against the papers on the table. "With someone as well read as you are, you should know, but if you need an explanation, a cad is a man who treats a woman poorly."

I thought about Luca trying to get his hands on the family book even back then and his actions definitely fit that category. "If he was such a loser, why did Aunt Mimi date him at all?"

"The word that was bandied about was *charming*. He knew what to say and how to say it, but all his sweet-talking ways didn't mean he was successful in getting his mitts on the family heirloom."

I pursed my lips and got up from the table, thinking as I walked into the bedroom, pulled the shades, and did the same in the office before going back into my room. Then I took the weathered leather-bound book, which to the casual observer resembled an old photo album, from the shelf and placed my hand on the cover. With my eyes closed, I focused my attention on the pages in my hand. The book began to warm under my touch. "Hidden in plain sight from prying eyes. And now for the surprise. Let the pages become visible to me. For this I wish so it shall be." I picked up the book and hugged it to my chest, thanking the sun, moon, and stars I had thought to protect my book, *Practical Beginnings*, with a spell. Even Milo hadn't known I had cast it and feeling proud, I went back to the kitchen.

He glanced at the book in my arms, and his eyes opened in surprise. "Where was that hiding?"

I wanted to poke fun at him, but he was my partner in my witch life, and I trusted him implicitly. "On my bookshelf."

His eyes widened, and he gave a nod of appreciation. "Oh, my dear witch, you are clever."

I bowed my head and didn't bother to keep the grin from filling my face. "I'm learning the tricks of this life."

"Aunt Mimi would be proud of you." He dipped his chin. "As am I."

"Thank you, Milo. Now let's see what our dusty old book has in store for us today."

I opened the book to the middle and waited while the pages flipped first toward the front and then in the direction of the back before it settled on a blank page. I closed it and opened it again before it repeated the same sequence of events. "That's odd. There is nothing on the page."

Milo sat down on the book, and I tried to push him off. "How can I try again if you've got your bum there?"

"This is a different kind of lesson." His voice was monotone. "Lily. This fight will be yours, and the book can't help you against the magician. But I promise you, that you will know what you need to do when the time comes and you won't be alone."

I blinked hard, astounded that my book wasn't offering any pearls of wisdom. "What good is a book of spells then? I might as well be learning how to drive a car without an instructor."

Milo shook his little head, his eyes round. If he had been human, I would have said he was worried. "I must have you make a promise."

This didn't sound good. I couldn't remember a time when my familiar demanded a promise from me. But I had no choice but to get him to continue his thought. "Go on."

"Until this person or persons are caught, you must not go anywhere alone. And even then, you might not have enough in your spell arsenal to come out unscathed. What you're about to embark on will test all your skills, even the ones you don't know you possess."

I was confused, and every day was a new challenge. I felt like a mermaid coming out of the ocean with legs that hadn't transformed yet. "How is this different than any other time I've searched for the bad guy?"

He dropped to the floor and began to walk from the room before looking over his shoulder. "It just is."

I slumped into a chair like a limp noodle. "Then how will I defend myself?" I was alone, asking questions that no one could answer. I thought of the spells I had learned and felt my confidence grow. In less than a year, I had gone from not even knowing I was a witch to being able to execute spells of protection, lighting a candle, causing things to disappear, and I could levitate objects and bring people and things to me. All of this I learned by reading and practicing. Sometimes it was easy, and other times it was excruciatingly hard, but I had done it all with support from Milo and the people who loved me. The only thing I wanted to do that I couldn't yet was fly. I didn't even have a broom yet, but it was on my bucket list, if a witch had such a list. But I had to trust the process, and when it was time to climb on a broom and soar, I would be able to.

T he next morning, I stumbled to the kitchen and poured myself a mug of coffee. I added a splash of cream and a spoonful of sugar. Milo wasn't anywhere to be found. So much for him having my back. But I wasn't upset. I was still coming up with a plan of attack today. I studied the images for the millionth time, and at some point during the night, I decided to concentrate on the last word. When I thought about five-letter words and looking back at the first five, each letter came from a full word. Using the same logic, I jotted down *M* and I felt the most common vowel used next would be *A*.

A sharp knock on the kitchen door drew my attention away from the pictures. I could see Nikki through the glass, and with a flick of my wrist, the door opened. She stepped inside and grinned.

"Good morning. Starting the day with a bit of magic." She slapped me a high five. "I had no idea you could open a door like that."

I snapped my fingers and said, "That's it." I grabbed a marker and under the last of the pictures, I wrote the letters *M, A, G, I, C*. I thrust my fist in the air and screamed, "Nikki, the last word is magic."

"You solved the puzzle? That's great." She rushed forward, and her brow furrowed. "What's the middle word?"

I shrugged my shoulders. "I'm not sure yet, but right now we have the first and third and for now, I'm okay with that." I held up the coffee mug. "Would you like a cup? And then I can tell you what my thoughts were for today."

She set a plate on the table. "I brought breakfast since I figured we were going to be on the go and needed a full belly to get us started."

"Make yourself at home. I'm going to get dressed; we have a bookstore to get to." I opened the back door and called for Milo. "Breakfast!" I closed the door and hurried down the hall, suddenly jazzed to get out there and clear my name.

By the time I got back to the kitchen, Milo was inhaling his kitty tuna from his bowl, and Nikki had set out breakfast wraps and chunks of fruit. "I hope you're hungry."

"Starved." And I meant it. I threw my arms around her and hugged her tight. "Thank you." The words came out strangled.

"Hey, what's this all about?" She continued to hug me.

Feeling overwhelmed and grateful for her rock-solid friendship, I released her. "You're a great Watson." It was our little joke that we were the dynamic duo of Sherlock Holmes and Dr. Watson.

"Well then, tell me exactly what we're going to do today. You know I love a plan."

I held up one finger. "Breakfast, the store, and we're going to walk through the scene while I put things back together. I also want to dissect what happened when they came into the store. Is it possible something has been over-looked? Because I don't think they are as powerful with magic as we are. And I also believe that my protection charm around this house was very strong. So we're going to break everything down until we figure out exactly how someone got the key to my store and my necklace. Once we know that, we'll be on our way to figuring out which one—Clay, Iris, or Celeste—did what and when."

Nikki clapped her hands together. "I love it when you get focused. It causes your magic to glow around you."

"Really? I've never seen your magic do that."

Laughing, she said, "Of course you haven't. I'm not as powerful as you are. Or did you forget that little tidbit?"

"All this talk of power and you have years of experience compared to me." I took one of the egg burritos, added a generous shot of hot sauce, and took a big bite. An explosion of taste from the spicy pepper jack cheese, smoky bacon, and creamy eggs danced on my tongue.

Milo paused in the middle of his breakfast and said, "Lily. Just accept that you're powerful and run with it. You're going to need everything in your spell book in the next thirty-six hours."

I paused before taking another bite. "Is there something you need to tell me, Milo? That is the second time you've insinuated things are going to get difficult before this is over."

His tail swished from side to side in short, agitated bursts. "That's all I can tell you. But trust your instincts."

I went back to inhaling my breakfast burrito. "Consider that you've done your job and warned me, but one of these days you're going to fess up and come clean about being clairvoyant."

"I'm not. It's called life experience."

And with that, Milo trotted out the kitty door. I wanted to call after him to see where he was going, but sooner or later, he'd show up again, and most likely it would be at the bookstore.

"I'm glad to be getting back into my routine, and with

any luck, William will have my favorite pecan cinnamon rolls today too."

"Are we taking the pictures and poster board to the shop?"

Picking up my wand, I pointed at the pages and whispered for them to become a stack on the table. It was a surprise when it happened, and I looked at Nikki as I grinned. "Magic is getting easier with each passing minute." I wasn't about to question the reason why all of a sudden it seemed to be easier than before. Milo and Nikki must be right about my powers coming on stronger since I was going to need them.

Nikki had tidied the kitchen in the same span of time and said, "Do you want me to drive today?"

"No, we'll take the Mini. We can get into tighter parking spaces than with your SUV." And I was about to remind her that she got nervous when we were following up on clues, so me behind the wheel was the best option.

"Good idea. Now, are we going back out to the motel today to confront your suspects?"

I paused and thought about what all I needed to discover, and I could feel my smile widen. "Oh, not to worry. We'll see each of them in turn today. I have a feeling once they realize I'm back at the shop, they'll find a reason to come by and"—I gave Nikki a saucy wink—"we'll be ready for them too."

"Is that when we'll figure out who the killer really is?" She held open the door as I slid the stack of papers into my tote bag and we hurried to the car.

"With any luck we'll know before the magicians show up, but if not, I have a feeling the guilty party won't be able to resist preening like a peacock."

"Over what exactly?" Nikki closed her car door, and I started the engine.

"They think their magic is strong, that Luca Rand taught them all the secrets to being powerful. And as they said, pride comes before the fall. Well, our guilty person's pride will cause them to fall right into a pair of handcuffs."

I backed into the street as my confidence continued to grow. "Nikki, what the magicians don't seem to understand is I am a witch, and magic is a part of me like breathing."

Chapter 18
Gage

Dax and I left Lily's bookstore early in the morning and went back to the police station, sitting in our respective offices. He had removed the spell that would keep everyone out. As promised, she was getting access to her shop, and I sent her a text letting her know she could come in at any time. A large part of me felt bad about the fingerprint powder that lingered on furniture and that she would have to clean the entire place from top to bottom, but it couldn't be helped. We had to do a thorough job investigating, but I didn't feel we were any closer to solving the crime than we were on day one. I couldn't remember a case where we had three excellent suspects but no real evidence tying them to the crime other than a hair clip and being co-workers. At worst, they had questionable taste in working with Rand. From what I'd been told, he was an unpleasant man. Too bad that wasn't a crime I could charge them with.

I slammed my fist on the top of my desk and muttered a few unpleasant words. Dax walked in holding two mugs of coffee. Handing me one, he sat in the chair across from me. "You're as frustrated as I am."

I thanked him for the coffee and took a sip. It was black as night and hot. Just what I needed to kick the brain cells in gear. "I feel like we're overlooking something, even a small clue, to get us moving in the right direction."

He rested his ankle on the opposite knee and looked out my window which had a clear view of the east end of the harbor. "I keep going over it, and the evidence brings me back to the same logical conclusion. Lily."

I slammed the mug on my desk, coffee sloshing over the sides, furious her name came out of his mouth. "You know she didn't kill Rand!"

He cocked a brow and held up his hand. "I didn't say that. Did the words Lily is guilty come out of my mouth and I missed it?"

His attempt to reassure me didn't work. "Not in so many words but you said it was the logical conclusion. And that's just as good as saying she did it."

"I know you're not going to like what I have to say, but it's good that Lily has decided to start looking around. She has a way of seeing things we as cops don't. Procedure and process are the way we operate, but Lily along with Nikki or even Milo, move in many directions where we plod forward."

Shaking my head, I said, "I don't like it. Exposing herself has turned out to be dangerous time and again." I glanced at my phone, half hoping she'd call and ask us to come to the store, but so far, there was silence. Had she even arrived there yet? Pushing back my chair, I half stood, and Dax gestured for me to sit.

"When she needs you, she'll call, but for now, Lily has to walk through her store and begin to put it back to rights.

It will also jolt her brain walking around the ribbon of books. She's doing great solving the first word, but the second and third are critical."

My backside connected with the chair, and even though I knew Dax was right, it grated on my nerves. We were engaged, and I wanted to help her in every way which included this mess. "The minute she calls or texts, I'm going over there."

Dax drank more of his coffee and waited for me to stop fidgeting. "And I'll go with you. But you remember what it was like on your first few stakeouts? Patience is the key to getting our man or woman."

Annoyed that he was right, I lifted my mug and took a drink, not that the caffeine would do anything to help settle me. "Patience is not something that I'm known for."

With a snort, he said, "Are you kidding? Your interrogations are legendary around here. The first week I was officially a member of the team, Peabody told me how you can sit in silence waiting for someone to crack and tell you everything you need to know."

A smile tugged at my mouth. "You shouldn't believe everything you hear around the water cooler."

"It was the coffee pot, and I've seen you in action too. You're good at the waiting game, but now we know that isn't true when it comes to investigations that involve someone you love."

Anxious to change the subject, I had been looking for an opportunity to dig more into Dax's life and background. "Tell me. When you asked Lily to have coffee, did you think a relationship would develop between the two of you?"

He grinned. "You mean while you and Lily were tap-dancing around your feelings and you both were strictly in the friend zone?"

I narrowed my eyes. "Did you do that deliberately to poke the green-eyed monster in me?"

"Possibly and look at you now, engaged to be married and planning a future together." He grew serious. "You shouldn't waste something special when you find it."

And that was the best opening I was going to get. "Is there or was there someone special in your life and she slipped through your fingers?"

He grew thoughtful. "No one specific but I know she's out there, and I was drawn to Maine for a reason. With patience, I'll find her, and hopefully, she will have been waiting for me too. I can tell you she's a witch."

"How do you know that?" There were so many layers to the witch life that I didn't understand.

He got up and stood by the window, and when he spoke, his voice softened and took on a reverent tone. "My mother told me from the time I was a young man that I would meet the woman I was meant to be with near the ocean, and she would be the opposite in looks. Where I'm dark-haired with dark eyes, she will be fair, and her eyes are the color of the northern Atlantic Ocean. The moment I lay eyes on her, I'll know."

I folded my hands on the top of the desk, contemplating what he had just said. The lack of specifics could mean she was anywhere on the coast, and there were a lot of women that were blonde with green eyes. "This means you were being my wingman, and I didn't even know it." I extended my hand. "You're a good friend, Dax."

After a hearty shake, he said, "Let's do a little old-fashioned foot patrol. If I was a betting man, Lily and Nikki have been hard at work for a while and there will be something that she wants to either ask or show us."

"Are you psychic now?" I happily pushed the chair

back, got up, and slipped my cell phone into the pocket of my dark pants.

"Not at all. Just observant, and if we don't start moving, you're going to take off running down Doenut Drive and end up at the Cozy Nook Bookshop. At least this way you won't come across as Lily's crazy fiancé."

"I'm going to grab gloves and a few evidence bags, just in case. Unlike you, I never underestimate Lily." He laughed his way out the door, and I figured I should do the same. Despite that I was sure we had done an excellent job searching the scene, Lily did have a way of discovering the unknown.

Once on the brick sidewalk, I longed to make a direct route to the bookstore, but Dax gestured to William's bakery, the Sweet Spot. "We should treat this like a normal day and pick up coffee and pecan buns or something equally delicious and also any tidbits that William might have about Luca Rand. You said yourself he lived in town for a while. Maybe William would remember something about him that is useful, and to sweeten the deal, I'll buy."

I looked in the direction of the bookstore, and my feet wanted to head in that direction, but my head agreed with Dax. A small but normal distraction would be what I needed. Reluctantly, I turned in the direction of the bakery. But from that front door to Lily's, I had an excellent line of sight. She was perfectly safe with Nikki and Milo with her at the shop. "Alright, but we should hurry."

He clapped a hand on my shoulder. "We're close by, she'll be just fine."

I pulled open the bakery door and expected to see

William, the older gentleman who had been running the bakery long before I came along, but behind the counter was Jill Dilly.

Her smile was wide and as bright as the midday sun. "Detective Erickson, Detective Peters. Good morning. What can I get you?"

"Jill, this is a surprise. When did you start working here?"

She blushed. "Gage, I thought you were on top of everything in this town. But since it's not a secret, William hired me a few weeks ago." She dropped her voice even though we were the only people in the bakery. "You know, after the unfortunate incident with Jerilyn and all."

Nodding solemnly, I said, "It's good to see you, and I know William can use the help. He's been stretched thin for quite some time now."

"Which is why this is perfect for both of us. I was hanging around without a purpose, and William needed someone." Again, she blushed, and I had to wonder if there was more going on here than a boss-employee relationship. However, if William wanted to share details, he would. I wasn't about to pry.

"I'm surprised Lily didn't mention it. She's been in since I started." She snapped open a white bakery bag. "Not that it matters. What can I get for you detectives today?"

Dax said, "We'll need a bakery box."

Jill beamed. "Even better." Putting the bag on the counter behind her, she got a large bakery box, and I chuckled. Dax mentioned the items he wanted from the case, and I added in four pecan cinnamon buns along with sugar cookies and two chocolate cupcakes. That should be enough sugar to keep Lily's energy up and Nikki's too.

She taped the box closed and handed it over the top of the case. "Coffee today?"

"Four, please." I jerked a thumb in Dax's direction. "And he's paying."

Being a good sport, he withdrew his wallet and handed her a credit card. "Jill, maybe you wouldn't mind answering a couple of questions for me."

She ran the card through the machine and handed it back to him. "Whatever I can do to help."

"You might have heard about the magician show that's going to be performed at the Lights Out Theatre?"

"I did, but I heard one of them died in Lily's shop." Her face screwed up in concern. "Poor Lily, to have someone break in and then die in her little store is just awful."

Dax nodded but kept going. "Did any of them happen to come into the bakery?"

"Oh yes, it was a few days ago. There were four of them, and then just yesterday it was the remaining three. They said they had been to Lily's too." She leaned forward. "If you ask me, those three aren't very broken up over what happened to their friend. But I heard them talking about Lily, saying how she killed him with a spell. Can you believe that? Grown people thinking a sweet girl like Lily could do such a thing?"

I wasn't sure if she meant cast a spell or kill a person and I didn't ask. Dax had the conversation under control.

"Is there anything else you can remember about the first time they came in?"

She chewed her bottom lip for a second. "Yes, the older man was talking about a book he wanted to get from Lily's store. Said it would complete his collection, and he kept twirling a loose button on his pea coat, muttering about having to sew it back on again."

"A pea coat?" Dax asked.

"This one looked to be authentic because the buttons had the anchor on it." She glanced at me and then back to Dax as if I could explain it further if necessary.

"And how do you know it was authentic?"

She punched a few keys on the cash register and withdrew a large round navy-blue button. "Because on the way out the door, this popped off. I tried to call after him, but he ignored me and headed in the direction of Lily's store. Since they were putting on a show, I guessed it would only be a matter of time until he came back in the bakery, and I could give it to him then."

"Would you mind if I took it?" Dax pulled out an evidence bag and held it out. "You can slip it right in here."

She did as asked and said, "Did I do something wrong?"

"Not at all, Jill. It's just that we're trying to discover if there was foul play involved in his death, and anything related to Mr. Rand and that day are important to our investigation."

Her face relaxed. "I'm always happy to help law enforcement. Who knew I had a clue this entire time just sitting in the cash register."

He leveled his gaze on her. "Please don't mention this to anyone except for William, of course. It's police business, and for now we should keep it confidential."

She ran a finger over her lips and said, "These are zipped."

"Is there anything else about the second time the magicians came into the shop?"

Again, she thought for several long moments. "The only thing I remember is the dark-haired woman say to the others that they had to stick together. It was when they were the strongest, oh and that Lily would get what was coming to her."

Dax glanced my way, and I shook my head. I didn't have any questions for Jill. He had extracted all that she knew, of that I was sure. And then I realized what she had said a moment ago. "Jill when you said they had been to Lily's, did they mean the store?"

"No. It sounded like they had just come from her house. Not that I asked, but the man said he didn't like how her cat sat on the fence watching them."

A stab of worry pierced my heart. Why hadn't Lily told me the magicians had been at her house yesterday?

"Jill, thank you for the pastry, coffee, and the conversation." Dax gave her a warm smile. "All have been most helpful."

"Anytime. We're open six days a week." She fluttered her fingertips in my direction. "Have a good day."

We said goodbye and didn't speak until we got to the middle of town square. It was always the best place to have a conversation since there were no shrubs or trees close enough for anyone to lurk behind, and no one could get close enough to overhear a single word.

"What do you make of that?" I asked.

Dax looked from right to left and then dropped his voice. "If they're stronger together, that means they were either talking about their magic or they're up to their top hats in this murder, together."

His thoughts mirrored mine. I began to walk through the grass in the direction of the bookstore, and Dax fell into step beside me. "Then our next step is to go to the bookstore and see if Lily has figured out the missing words and to find out why she never mentioned they were at her house."

Chapter 19
Lily

Standing outside my back door, I bent down to retrieve a large navy button. Holding it up so that I could take a closer look, I said, "Nikki, it has an anchor on it, and it must have come from a coat."

She peered over my shoulder "My dad used to have a wool coat. He got it from a thrift store, and it had those kinds of buttons. He called it his pea coat."

"Do you know anyone who has one now?" I turned it over and looked at the back side. It wasn't caked with dirt so it hadn't been outside long. But who could have dropped it?

So far, we had thoroughly searched the kitchen slash storage room and now the back entrance and all we found was a solitary button. I closed the door after we went back inside and placed the button next to the cash register. "I've been thinking about the book titles, and I'm tempted to pick them up."

"What's stopping you?" Nikki settled into one of the wingback chairs near the front windows, legs crossed with her hand on her midsection. She laughed as her stomach gurgled, and I glanced at the clock above the door. "Sorry."

"A few more minutes and then we'll figure out what we'll do for lunch." Leaning on the counter, I looked around my bookstore. Even though I could levitate the bookcase back into place, I wasn't ready to do it. I wanted to see if I could get in the mind of the killer. "Why would someone have brought their own step stool to the store? I had a ladder."

"Maybe they were trying to not be as tall so anyone passing by the shop wouldn't see them?"

I snapped my fingers. "Or what if the person was tall and didn't need the ladder but a small stool would suffice when shearing the bolts off." I walked to where I had set up the ladder and moved it to the side before adding a box with the step stool dimensions to the space. It would have been handy if Dax had left the stool here, but the box would do for this exercise. I hurried back to the kitchen and found a tape measure and checked the distance between the top of the box and eye level to the bolts. "Eighty-five inches."

Nikki said, "What does that tell us?"

I whirled around. "The height of the person who cut the bolts." I gave her a triumphant grin and finally felt as if I was getting my mojo back. "The box is eighteen inches. From the step to the bolts is another sixty-five inches. If we're putting them at eye level that means the killer is roughly six feet tall. Which rules out Iris or Celeste from loosening the bolts."

"While they're tall, maybe not six feet, they could have worn platform shoes."

That was a good point so I'd need to take a look at their closets to verify, but I couldn't picture a woman standing on a stool in platform shoes loosening the bolts off. It made more sense that this was a man. So now I was pointing the proverbial finger at Clay Proctor. He was about the right height, and it fit.

"Alright, so ruling out the women for loosening the bookcase and going back to your theory they were working together, what were the women doing while Clay was loosening the bolts?"

"Searching for the book or placing these books to leave me a clue." I set the ladder up and climbed on. Looking at the covers from this vantage point, I was hoping something would leap out at me, but there wasn't a discernable pattern to them.

"Anything come to mind?" Nikki asked, still relaxing in the chair.

I glanced her way. "Come take a look, and see what you think." I got down, and she took my place. "What do you see?"

Wrinkling up her nose, she tipped her head to the right and then to the left. "Honestly? Nothing but I'm not good at puzzles; that's your thing." She got down, and the tapping on the door drew my attention away from the puzzle.

A smile replaced the frown I know had been plastered on my mouth. I stepped over the books and hurried to open the door to let Gage and Dax inside. They had a tray of to-go cups that bore the Sweet Spot logo and a bakery box. "Nik, we've got sustenance."

She was right behind me, eager to get her hands wrapped around a cup. As I opened the door, wonderful aromas wafted up, and my mouth began to water. Whatever was in the box would be delicious, and the coffee a welcome addition.

"Gage. Dax. This is a surprise. We didn't expect to see you." They came in, and I closed the door. Gage looked around the room.

"You haven't gotten much done. I thought for sure the store would be put back together, or do you need help?" He flexed his bicep and grinned. "I can put some muscle behind my words."

I snagged two cups of coffee and handed one to Nikki, and we popped off the lids at the same time and sipped. "This hits the spot."

"Did you run out of coffee?" Dax asked. "Or is this just better?"

I smiled over the rim of the cup. "First, no one makes a better cup of coffee than William, and we've been busy and just haven't gotten around to brewing any."

Gage cocked an eyebrow. "Busy?"

I waved for the guys to sit down, and Dax pulled up his usual chair. Gage grabbed the stool behind the desk, so Nikki and I could have the wingback chairs.

I looked between the men and said, "Here's my idea, and before you interrupt, hear me out." Pausing to make sure they would let me talk, I waited for Gage specifically to indicate he would remain silent, at least for a few minutes.

"When you can't find your way through a tunnel, sometimes the best route you can take is to turn around and start back from the beginning, see where you took a wrong turn." I made a sweeping gesture with my arm. "And this is the beginning. From the moment Luca and his friends walked into my store, the wheels were in motion."

Dax said, "Go on."

"Before we discuss about the first time we met, I want to tell you what we've discovered today." I got up and retrieved the button we found. Handing it to Dax, since he was the lead investigator, I said, "We found this by the back door this morning. It's from a pea coat. Most likely it popped off someone's coat when they came in the back door, but since

I'm the only person who comes and goes that way and I don't own a pea coat, it has to belong to the killer."

Handing it to Gage, he said, "What else did you find?"

I looked him in the eye. "Whoever loosened the bolts was around six feet tall which means the women couldn't have; they're too short and would have had to overreach." I quickly explained the measurements I had taken and said, "Based on how tall the stool was and the bolts being at eye level, it had to have been Clay. But I intend on checking to see if either woman has platforms since that could change everything as far as being tall enough."

Gage nodded and said, "Good piece of detective work. Too bad we didn't think about that. Even after you told us the stool wasn't yours, we didn't go any further in our thought process, only that the bolts had been loosened using magic."

Dax said, "Do you remember anyone wearing a coat like what you've described into the store in the last week or so? Maybe someone slipped out the back when you weren't looking."

I shook my head. "I would have remembered if someone had done that. Besides, Nikki was here, and she saw them leave through the front too. I recall Luca and Iris were wearing blue coats. I don't recall if one wore a pea coat."

Gage looked at Dax, and he glanced at the floor. Now I was more than curious about this button. "What do you know that we don't?"

Dax said, "Nothing I can tell you as it's part of an ongoing investigation."

"Is it about the button?" I focused my attention on Dax since he was running things at the moment.

"Lily, I can't say one way or the other."

Slapping my hand on the arm of the chair, I said, "Now

that we've established there's something to do with a button, was Luca wearing that coat when he was found?" I closed my eyes, trying to think about what he had on when I found him. "No. He wasn't wearing a coat; I remember he had on a sweater. Which means he had to have removed it when he broke into the store. But we didn't find it, so that means someone took it when they left. Our killer."

Giving Nikki a look, I said, "We'll need to track down the coat." Excitement once again began pulsing through my veins. I was onto something important, and by the look on the guys' faces, they knew it too. "Since your investigation seems to be on the slow boat, how about we play a word game? I'll ask a question, and if I'm wrong you can say, no comment, but if I'm right, you don't say anything at all."

Nikki gave me a quick wink. It was good that she was always ready to keep digging into unknown territory to ferret out the truth.

Since neither Gage nor Dax disagreed with my idea and Nikki was all ears, I began, but each question needed to be carefully worded. "Do you believe this button is connected to Luca Rand's death?"

Silence.

"Do you have reason to believe Luca was wearing a pea coat with a button like this one?"

I began to grin as the guys didn't speak again.

"Have you searched Luca's room for the coat that matches the button?"

Dax said, "No comment."

"Alright, so we do need to track down the coat."

I needed another yes or no question. "Do you know who killed him?"

This time Gage said, "No comment."

Which I took as a solid no. I felt my shoulders sag. This

Q and A wasn't really getting me anywhere. "Look, let's stop playing around. You need to go find that coat, and we'll solve the puzzle with the book titles. We can meet up later and compare notes."

Gage's brows peaked above his eyes. "Are you suggesting we go out to the motel and go through Rand's room again?"

I got up and smiled. "That is an excellent idea. If you find something, you can send me a text and our code word will be *silent*."

Nikki got up too and said, "I think I have an idea about the next word so we really should get back to it."

Dax leaned back in his chair. "I'm not buying this, Lily. You're up to something, and for yours and Nikki's safety, you should fill us in."

I pulled Gage to his feet, and Nikki did the same with Dax before I pointed to the door. "Time is wasting and besides, I already gave you two clues, the button, and the height of the murderer. So it's your turn to find some information that you can share with us." I tapped my pointer finger on my chin. "While you're there, you should talk with the other three. Focus your attention on Clay; he's the logical choice."

Gage said, "First tell me why you neglected to mention you had visitors yesterday morning?"

I felt the color drain from my face. "How did you find out?" Before he could answer, I waved my hand. "It doesn't matter. It was no big deal. They were just trying to push my buttons and discovered I'm not a pushover."

He narrowed his eyes. "Is there anything else you forgot to mention that you say is no big deal?"

"Well, just one more little thing. When we were here yesterday and you asked me to sit in the chair, I might have moved it four inches so I could have a better view of the scene of the crime." I used my hands to show him how much I moved the chair. "But that's it, I promise."

Nikki graciously opened the door, and Milo slunk in and proceeded to hop onto his cushion in the window.

He swished his tail from right to left. "Are Detective Cutie and our newest witch going someplace?"

I went around to Gage's backside and placed my hands on his upper back, pushing him to the door. "Yes, they're going to the motel to check for a pea coat. I'll explain it all to you after they've gone."

He tipped his head to one side and grumbled, "Good. We can get back to solving the—" He stopped talking as Dax took note of his words. "Puzzle."

"Milo, is that what you were really going to say?" Dax asked.

Gage groaned. "I wish I understood what Milo was saying. Dax, you've got all the luck being a witch."

Milo looked at Gage. "It's not that big of a deal."

His comment left me and Nikki chuckling as we finally got the guys out the door and it closed. I wiped my brow as if that had been a hard job. "Whew, now we can get down to business."

Nikki said, "I don't have any idea what the next word of the word jumble is."

"Oh, don't worry about that. I'm going to call the motel and ask our three suspects to come down to the store. I'll push their buttons by telling them I know that one of them is responsible for Luca's death. That should give them some motivation."

She looked at the closed door. "Then why did we send our backups to the motel if we're bringing the suspects here? That's a bit backward, don't you think?"

I crossed my arms over my chest and grinned. "Nope because by the time they get here, we'll have a plan, and as witches, we can contain them until Gage and Dax can get back to town. Remember, Nik, they're magicians not witches so they don't have a wide range of magic at their disposal like we do." I crossed the short distance to where Milo was sitting and scooped him up. "And don't forget we have the most important part of defeating them right here."

Milo's head swiveled as he looked around the room. "I hope you're not referring to me. I'm just a familiar."

I laughed out loud. "Hardly. I'm beginning to suspect you have more magic in the swish of your tail than Nikki and I have put together."

He shook his head. "My dear witch, you have your wand and your powers; that is all you'll need."

I winked at Nikki. "Not acknowledging the question is the answer I needed."

Chapter 20
Lily

I paced behind the counter and casually shot a glance in Nikki's direction. "I'm going to toss out some stuff that is pure conjecture, and lacking real evidence, it only makes sense. We need to go back to when Luca came into the bookstore. He was ready to take my book of magic after Iris pointed it out. Then you arrived and basically did that Wonder Woman thing, and they backed down and left. But we know they wanted the book. Flash forward to the end of my workday."

"Hold on there." She walked over to me and positioned me behind the counter. Taking two books, she placed them on the counter with a space apart. "Pretend these books represent Iris and Luca. Where are Clay and Celeste? In an aisle? If they had been near the historical section, it would have been easy for one of them to slip into the other room, especially when Iris was chatting you up."

I turned to my left. "I thought they came from over here." And the question niggled at my brain. "Could they have snuck into the back room while we were talking?"

Nikki nodded and her mouth was thin. "What if one of them found your house keys and took an impression to break in later."

"But why?" I leaned on the counter, my chin resting in my cupped hands as my elbows held me up.

"Luca Rand came to the bookstore with one mission, to find the book. It wouldn't surprise me to learn he knew exactly who you were and maybe part of his plan the entire time was to take the keys so he could search your house while you were at work."

That made sense. "If we're going down this path, then why come to my house and take my necklace?"

She shook her head. "I don't have an answer for that one. But I don't think they broke through your protection spell at home since the key allows access. He walked right in, protections holding steady."

"Taking the key to my house makes sense, but whoever did that obviously messed up by not taking an impression of the shop key too. That has to be why he had to risk coming to my house." I straightened and a slow smile grew. "We might have enough to bait the trio of magicians now."

Milo hopped onto the counter. "Lily, baiting them is not a good idea without Dax and Gage being close by."

I picked him up and held him close before kissing the top of his soft gray head. "Milo, are you starting to like having Gage and Dax around?"

"I wouldn't go that far, but they do serve a purpose from time to time." He squirmed in my arms, and I gently set him on the floor. He didn't stalk off as I expected but said, "If you're determined to go through with your headstrong plan, I'll be around. Just in case."

I was beginning to wonder if he doubted my abilities to

solve the case. Before I let Milo really get in my head, I called the motel.

Torrie answered in a bright cheery voice, "Coastal Motel, how may I help you?"

"Hi, Torrie, this is Lily Michaels, and I was hoping you could connect me to Iris Herman's room."

"I wish I could, but Iris and her friends went out earlier. When they stopped in the office to get coffee, she said they were going to the theatre to run through the show. Clay said something about having lunch at the Copper Kettle. They only left a half hour ago so you should be able to catch them there."

"Thanks for the information, Torrie."

"Anytime."

I set the phone on the counter and said to Nikki, "How would you like to run over to the Copper Kettle and see if you can plant an idea that Iris, Clay, and Celeste should stop here before going to the theatre."

"I can, but shouldn't you let Gage and Dax know what you're up to?"

I could hear the caution in her voice and rushed to reassure her. "We're just going to talk. I won't poke them too hard with my wand."

Nikki tipped her head and gave me that side-eye look as if she didn't believe me. Before she could leave the store, the trio we had been talking about were standing outside my shop door. She went to unlock it and ushered them in.

"Hello." I gave each one a smile. "What brings you over today?" I was sincere in asking my question, but the dour expressions they wore didn't bode well that this was a social call. Iris was clenching and unclenching her right hand; Celeste's head swiveled right and left as if checking to see if we were alone, and Clay strode in my direction.

"We've come to get answers to our questions."

Iris and Celeste's heads bobbed in agreement.

Celeste said, "That's right. What did Luca ever do to you that was so bad you had to kill him?"

I could feel my brow shoot to my hairline. "That's very interesting. I wanted to ask you the same question."

Nikki shut the door, and Milo hopped up onto the counter next to me, waiting to see what was about to come next.

Clay took a menacing step closer and placed his balled-up fists on the counter. He was less than a foot from me and could easily reach out and strangle me. Not that he would. First, Nikki and Milo were with me, and would he really resort to physical violence? I had many questions that needed answers.

"He wanted your book, and to protect it, you killed him." Iris's voice had a razor-sharp edge.

"The book wouldn't have done him any good. Only a Michaels witch can read it."

A look of disbelief crossed Celeste's face. "Not true. Luca found an old book, and he learned its secrets. One of them was how to read any magical book that was unreadable to others."

A chill raced down my spine. If this was true, magic could fall into the hands of people who didn't follow our code of ethics—do no harm. "Why did he want it?"

Clay said, "He wanted to be the best and most famous magician in the world. Your family's book is legendary. The power it contains would have done that."

"Let's think about your comment for a minute. I'm a Michaels witch. Don't you think my book would have all kinds of protections around it? Even if Luca had gotten his hands on it, he couldn't have broken them."

Nikki never blinked. She knew it was only after all of this craziness that I protected my book, home, and shop. But she would never betray my secret.

Celeste hovered near the wingback chairs. "Then why did you kill him?"

The anguish in her blue eyes was crystal clear. She believed that I was responsible. "Maybe you should ask Clay or Iris."

Clay's fist connected with the counter, and the sound jarred my teeth. "I'm done listening to you protest your innocence. Luca came here because you called and lured him here with the promise of selling him the book. He said you were losing money on the bookstore and selling that book would get you out of a bind."

"Who stole a copy of my house key? Was it you who broke in and stole my necklace?"

Celeste blanched, and she glanced at Clay. "She knows."

His head snapped in her direction. "She knows nothing. Keep quiet."

She took a step back, cowering from the anger emanating from him.

He turned his focus to Milo, staring as if trying to force him to do something without saying a word.

Milo flicked his tail and whimpered softly, "Lily. Help," and he went limp.

I pulled him into my arms, and I could feel his heart beating as I silently wrapped protection around us both. I wasn't sure what Clay was trying to do and hoped Nikki would realize she needed to protect herself as well.

Clay focused his attention on me. A look of surprise and then awe crept over his face. "Nicely done, but I have ways of getting you to confess the truth."

He threw his hands into the air, and books began to fly off the shelves, creating a tornado-like effect, and one mini cyclone was rapidly moving in Nikki's direction. Before I could say anything, two more kicked up and were wreaking havoc in the store. Chairs were breaking into splinters; shelves were toppling over; even a few plants dropped to the floor, shattering into piles of dirt and greenery.

A sneer appeared on Clay's face. "Shall I keep going? Or are you ready to give me the book? But, of course, that's after you tell us the truth about why you killed Luca."

My heart was crushed as I watched my beautiful shop being destroyed before my eyes. I gave Milo a kiss and gently placed him on the counter. It was time to show them who they were dealing with. With a flick of my wrist, the tornados stopped spinning and books fell to the floor.

Iris snapped her fingers, and I looked in her direction. She was holding up a long thin piece of wood and it was burning. "Confess or this shop is going up in flames."

Celeste shook her head. "And it would be a shame." From her bag, she withdrew a wand and pointed it at Nikki who then slumped to the floor. I didn't have time to process that Celeste was a witch and had just used her wand against another.

How could I get the fire out or prevent Iris from dropping it? Before I could solve that problem, Clay set the book tornados in motion once again, and now with the books twirling, an open flame, and Nikki and Milo incapacitated, I was on my own. The odds weren't great at three against one.

I drew myself up and faced Iris first; the threat of a fire burned in my veins. I knew how to light a candle, so I concentrated and willed my breath to reverse the spell. Holding out my hand and picturing water pooling in it, I said, "Extinguish the flame that threatens thee. Fire come to me. This I wish so it shall be." Like a flaming arrow, the stick Iris had held plunged into the palm of my hand and hissed to a wisp of smoke. Ignoring the searing pain from the fire, I glanced first at Clay who was using his energy to keep the books aloft, and it was then I realized the bigger danger came from Celeste who had turned her wand on me.

"You've guessed my secret. I'm not really a magician. I was tossed from my coven and had to find new"—she tipped her head from side to side—"friends." Her eyes were cold, and her smile was frozen in place. "Luca was such a drag. Thinking he could actually perform magic. Once he told us about his plan to get your book, I had to pretend to be a struggling magician and tag along."

She flicked the wand in Clay's direction, and he sank to the floor the same way Nikki had, and she repeated the gesture at Iris. "Now, this is the way it should have always been, just two powerful witches coming together, wand against wand."

This was not the twist I was expecting, and how was I going to protect not just myself, but the shop, three people, and my familiar? "Maybe you can clear a few things up for me since we've come to a showdown."

Without lowering her wand a fraction of an inch, she said, "Don't underestimate me, but I can indulge you for a few minutes, I guess. Then I must have the book and be on my way."

I wanted to start with some easy questions to get her to lower the wand slowly so conversation was my best weapon at this point. And I needed answers even though it was obvious that Celeste had killed Luca and was planning on killing me next. As I stood in front of this murderer, I thought of the books carefully arranged on the floor, and the clue finally clicked. With conviction that I had figured it out I asked, "Whose idea was it for the books to be lined up with the phrase *Never Underestimate Magic*."

She laughed. "Iris had a hand in that one. She fancies herself a clever magician." Jerking her thumb in the direction of the woman slumped to the floor, she said, "Very talented, don't you think?"

A tremor raced through me. "Why take the keys?"

"Lily, why don't you tell me your theory, and I'll fill in the blanks. We've done some poking around town since we arrived, and it turns out you're some kind of puzzle queen. I'll bet you have most of this figured out by now."

I glanced at the windows.

Celeste sneered. "Oh, and don't worry. No one from the outside can see what's going on in here. To the passersby, it looks like you have a few customers browsing."

At least if Gage and Dax came back to town, they'd know something was wrong. That gave me a small measure of comfort, but until then it was up to me. "Well, given the new wrinkle about your true abilities, I'd say Luca always wanted my family's book. It whet your appetite, and since a witch outside a coven would need more power to survive, it was the perfect opportunity for you."

"That's a rehash of what I already told you." She yawned. "Stop boring me. You can do better."

"Clay made an impression of my house key."

She waved her wand in a slashing motion through the air. Her lip curled into a sneer. "Nope, I did that, and in full transparency, neither Clay nor Iris can do any magic. It was all me. I gave them the illusion of power. Can you believe they really thought they could cast spells, like causing a tornado in the store or creating fire?"

At least I was only dealing with one witch. "Okay, well, Luca entered my house and somehow got my necklace."

She shook her head this time. "Wrong again. You're really not good at puzzles. People have you mixed up with someone else. That was me too. Luca didn't have the skill to get your protection necklace, but I did use the key to avoid having to deal with your house spell. By the way, it was quite good. I was mildly impressed."

Not that I needed her praise, but it was good to hear that it was decent even if I hadn't boosted it properly. "Why did Luca want to kill me?"

Her eyes gleamed. "Now you're doing better, but how did you know it was Luca?"

"He's the only one tall enough to loosen the bolts, and while he was doing that, Iris set up the book clue. Did he intend to lure me here and push the bookcase over?"

Celeste clapped her hands together. "Finally. And I left your necklace to implicate you. Luca had to die so I could have the book. These two came along to do some of the dirty work, but they didn't know the plan was for anyone to die, let alone Luca. They've been following him around like he's the Pied Piper and the route to fame and fortune." She withdrew a large black book from her bag. "Now it's time for the switch. Here is the new version of *Practical Beginnings*. Now if you'd be so kind as to hand over the original, I'll leave you to deal with these murder suspects."

"Do you really think I'll just hand over my book because you're holding me at wand point?"

"It's not you that I'll harm." She nodded to the counter where Milo lay. "But I do think you'll sacrifice everything for your familiar." Then she flicked the wand in Nikki's direction. "Or even her."

My heart stilled. I had to buy time. "The book isn't here. You can come with me, and I'll give it to you."

"Oh, Lily. I've been around the cauldron a time or three. Given the circumstances, you would never have the book far from reach. Now be a good beginner witch and give me the book or your friend is first, and if that doesn't motivate you, the familiar will be next."

My mind raced with possible spells, but nothing I had learned so far applied. And then I remembered Milo telling me pure and good intention was all that was needed for the strongest of spells. First, I needed a distraction while I came up with one. Placing a hand on Milo, I felt his body moving up and down. He was still breathing. Energy surged from his fur into my fingertips.

I reached under the desk and pulled out my book and set it on the countertop and then put Milo on top of it. Celeste took a step closer and the wand dipped as she stretched out her other hand to touch it. Sparks flew from the book, zapping her, and I jerked the wand from her hand. Surprise followed by anger filled her face and then rage.

"A wand is just a tool."

I held it aloft and said, "Magic turn on the wand. Make it crack and begone. This I wish so shall it be." The wand crumbled into pieces and disappeared from sight.

Celeste screamed, "What have you done?" Her arms shot up, fingertips to the sky. "You will pay for that."

The front windows rattled, and the door burst open just as I yelled, "No." Clapping my hands together, her arms crossed over her head and she was unable to move.

Gage and Dax burst through the door, and as Gage rushed to my side, Dax magicked handcuffs on Celeste's wrists. I pointed to Nikki. "Dax, help her."

I focused my attention on Milo, gently picking him up

and holding him close. Looking at Gage with tears in my eyes, I whispered, "I need Aunt Mimi."

He brushed the wetness from my cheeks. "She's on her way." He guided me to a chair, and I sat down. Nikki was opening her eyes as Dax watched over her.

"What happened?" She saw Milo in my arms. "Is he going to be okay?"

Aunt Mimi's voice boomed. "Yes."

"Aunt Mimi, Celeste is a dark witch, and she was the one who wanted the book the entire time. I don't know what she did to Milo, but he's been like this for a long time."

My tears slipped from my eyes, but it felt like they were being ripped from my heart. As they fell on Milo's fur, Aunt Mimi placed a hand on his tiny head. She looked into my eyes. "You can heal him. Believe in yourself."

"Familiars are immortal. Why isn't he waking up?" I buried my face in his fur and cried. Everyone else ceased to exist. I had to get to my book and find the right spell to save him, but I needed to be able to see so I let the tears flow from the depth of my soul, until they began to slow.

I gathered him closer to me, and I heard in a strained but familiar kitty grumble, "Hey, you're smooshing me."

"Milo!" I held him out and then repositioned him on my lap. "Are you really awake and talking?"

"Of course. You didn't think a little thing like black magic could slow me down, did you?" He reached up and patted my wet cheeks. "Thanks for these."

"Crying all over your fur." I wiped my cheeks with the back of my hand. "I know how much you pride yourself on looking handsome at all times."

"No, my dear witch, your tears are what saved me."

Gage crouched next to us and slipped his arms around my shoulders and scratched between Milo's ears.

My familiar sighed. "The most powerful magic is love and family."

I looked at Dax, Nikki, and Aunt Mimi, and I kissed the top of Milo's soft head and then kissed Gage. "And we are a family."

A week later the Cozy Nook Bookshop was open for business. The three magicians had been arrested, and another case was solved. I had stopped at the Sweet Spot earlier in the day to pick up a very special cake, and now I was waiting for Gage to arrive and have coffee time with me.

The bell on the front door jingled, and I winked at Milo who was stretched across the counter. I whispered to him, "It's time."

"Good luck. But I don't think you'll need it."

I ruffled the top of his head before greeting Gage with a kiss and a huge grin.

"I'm so glad you had some time to come over for coffee. William is trying out cake flavors. He needs taste testers, so I volunteered us."

He hugged me and pulled me into his lap as we sat in his favorite chair. "I'm always up for a slice of cake. Hopefully, we have coffee too."

I laughed. "Of course, I know what my fiancé likes." I handed him a knife, and he took it. "Care to do the honors?" I picked up the small cake plate and held it in front of him.

He placed the knife across the top of the cake and began to slice through the center. A frown appeared on his face. "There's a lump in there."

I set the plate on the small table and stood up. "Finish

cutting it so we can see what's inside." I handed him a small plate so he could put cake on it.

He made another cut so it was one fourth of the original size and slid the oversized slice to the plate. "What's this?" From the layer of frosting, he pulled two rings tied together with purple ribbon. "We need to get this back to William; he gave us someone else's cake."

I dropped to my knees, took the rings from him, and held his hand. "No, he didn't. I wanted to ask you to marry me on September fifth and I thought, if you like the rings I picked out and the cake, you might say yes."

A look of surprise and then ecstasy stared back at me. "Are you kidding? I'd marry you tomorrow if you asked. But September is good too." He stood and swept me into his arms. "You just made me the happiest man on earth."

Milo grumbled from the counter, "Looks like we've got a non-magical moving in soon."

Gage laughed as he looked at Milo. "I'm not sure what you said, but I'm going with 'welcome to the family.'"

I cupped his cheek, and before kissing him, I said, "Milo is right; love and family are the most powerful magic of all."

If you loved Magicians & Murder help other readers find this book: **Please leave a review now!**
Are you ready to read more from the Lily and the gang in Pembroke?
Keep reading for a sneak peek at
Artifacts & Amulets
A Book Store Cozy Mystery Series

Order Now
Or

Shop at Lucinda Race

Not ready to stop reading yet? If you sign up for my newsletter at www.lucindarace.com/newsletter you will receive an excerpt for Cookies & Capers, the introduction of when Lily met Milo right away as my thank-you gift for choosing to get my newsletter.

Artifacts & Amulets

LUCINDA RACE

Chapter One

Lily

The door to the Cozy Nook Bookshop opened with a sharp bang. A man, about fifty, with streaks of gray in his hair and mustache, scowled at me. He wore a crisp brown suit with a white shirt and orange tie that reminded me of a pumpkin. The woman was a bit younger, wearing a dark skirt, matching jacket, and a pale blue blouse, making her deep blue eyes more pronounced, and three-inch heels. Her hair was coiffed in a short, no-nonsense style that complimented her face. She closed the door and glanced around, her face expressionless.

"Welcome to my bookstore. I'm Lily. If there is anything I can help you find, please ask."

The man gave a curt nod of acknowledgment as the woman stepped to the counter. I was perched on a wooden stool and put aside my family's book on magic, *Practical Beginnings*, that I had been reading.

"Is there a specific book you're looking for today?"

She glanced at the man and back at me. "I am. A book on amulets. Do you have anything in stock?"

I gave her a wide smile. "Yes." I stood and headed down the aisle close to where my familiar, Milo, was snoozing on the window seat. The sun streamed in the large plate glass windows, bathing his gray fur in warmth. He lifted his head and looked at the customer through slits in his eyes before he bolted to an upright position.

I smiled at the couple. "Did you know there is an exhibit at the Olde Town Library with artifacts that include several amulets? Their history is reported to be quite interesting."

The man said, "Why do you think we're in town? We forgot our reference books in the city, so show us what you have and stop jaw-jacking."

I didn't appreciate his cantankerous tone but the old saying the customer is always right had me tamping down a sharp retort. I gestured to the shelf in front of them as if we were on a game show and I was the hostess showing off the gifts. "Here you go. As you can see there are several. I hope you find what you're looking for."

The woman tipped her head. "Thank you."

She turned her back to me as if I shouldn't see what book she picked up first. I took the hint that I was dismissed and took my time going back to the counter. The couple didn't seem to be enjoying their day, and I found this curious. Outside, the sun was bright; temperatures were pleasant for a June day, and from what I had heard, the exhibit at the library was fascinating. I caught Milo staring at me, and I gave him a wink. If he wanted to talk to me, he could, non-magicals would only hear him meow. He hopped to the floor, leaving one of his favorite napping spots, and trotted behind me. I picked him up and set him on the counter.

While Milo and I waited, the woman's voice was laced

with agitation. "I must see the Heart of the Soul amulet. It is imperative my proposal is accepted."

Nodding in their direction, I whispered, "What do you think their problem is?"

In a deep kitty growl, Milo said, "Be careful. I'll explain later."

I was surprised to see him continue to stare in the customers' direction. He was engrossed by their conversation. I arched a brow in his direction, but he ignored me and swished his tail in a jerky side to side motion.

After several long minutes, the couple carried a stack of books to the desk. The woman sorted through the titles, handing five to the man and placing one on the table behind them. With a thud, he set them on the counter next to Milo. "We'll take these."

"If you need directions to the library, it's on the corner of Doenut Drive and Route 1 on the right, at the end. But if you'd prefer to walk you can cut through the town square and get there in a few minutes."

"Good to know."

I rang up the books and gave him the total, but the woman handed me her credit card. I glanced at the name as the transaction was being processed. "Petra. That's a beautiful name."

"Dr. Addington." She wrenched the card from my hands. "Can I sign for the purchase please?"

My eyes widened at her rudeness, but she wouldn't be the last customer with an attitude when they entered my shop. As I slipped her books into a brown paper bag, I looked past her to see what the man was doing.

He was reading the back jacket of the book Petra had set aside.

"Simon. The bag." Without so much as a thank you, she

turned in her pumps and strode to the door, her heels clacking against the wood floor.

The man, who I now knew as Simon, shrugged. "The boss," and he trailed after her, looking more like a sad puppy than a grown man.

The door closed with much less force than when it was opened, and I watched Petra and Simon get into a heated exchange. Petra's arms were flailing about, and she repeatedly jabbed him in the middle of his chest. He stepped back while she advanced on him, still carrying on. I wished the windows were open so I could hear what they were saying.

"You know, my dear witch, if you hadn't been slacking on your studies, you might have discovered the spell for eavesdropping. Typically, it's frowned upon in our coven. However, there are circumstances in which rules could be interpreted that it was warranted, especially when it's easy to see she is extremely agitated." He tipped his head back and watched me, watching the action outside.

"What do you know about the Heart of the Soul? I've never heard of it."

"It's an amulet." He quickly jumped to the floor and trotted into the back room.

That short answer wasn't like Milo. "Where are you going?"

"Out." He pushed on the kitty door and left it swinging in his wake.

I crossed my arms over my chest and then looked at the sidewalk. Petra and Simon were gone. If I hadn't been distracted, I could have seen in which direction they went. Glancing at the desk calendar, I was pleased to realize the library was open late tonight. With a quick text to my fiancé, Detective Gage Erikson of the Pembroke Police Department, I let him know I'd be stopping at the library after I closed the store. I smiled at the idea of spending time at the library in spite of Milo's rude departure.

What was it today with rudeness? I sank to the stool. My eyes were drawn to the kitty door. Where had he gone?

I placed my hand on the old leather-bound book in front of me~~ I placed my hand on the cover~~ and closed my eyes. I focused on Milo, and the cover warmed under my touch. The tug of concern to make sure my familiar was safe increased. I opened the book. Pages began to turn, first right and then left until it lay open. I read the title of the spell; *Stay Connected to Your Familiar*. This was just what I needed. I continued to read aloud. *To create a deeper connection between a witch and her familiar, recite this spell.* Under my breath I said:

Two peas in a pod are we.

For when I need to see what you can see.

Not to be used frivolously.

This I wish, and so it shall be.

After I had read through it once, I read it out loud again with more conviction in my voice. I crossed to the front window and looked across the town square, hoping to catch a glimpse of my gray fur ball. But he was nowhere to be seen. I was tempted to use the summoning spell. Instead, I closed my eyes and repeated the connection spell again. This time, I could see the front doors of the library from the elevation of the sidewalk. Was it possible I could see what Milo saw at this very moment?

In my vision, I saw a leaf skitter across the sidewalk, but the focus on the front doors never wavered. He knew how to get inside if that was what he wanted. I waited another couple of minutes before I opened my eyes. The urge to know what was going on was stronger than before. For now, I'd bide my time. In a moment of clarity, I decided Milo would go with me to the library tonight. There was more than one way to get to the bottom of things.

An hour later Milo slunk around the corner of a bookcase. I watched him out of the corner of my eye as he paused and then sat down. "My dear witch, can we talk?"

"Always." I gestured to the wingback chairs positioned near the front window. It was one of my favorite places to curl up. Often, I enjoyed a hot beverage and read when time permitted or shared coffee and a sweet treat with Gage or whoever else might stop in.

With a tentative gait, he walked to one of the chairs and jumped up. A band constricted my heart. Whatever was going on with Milo had me on edge. He never moved at a sedate pace. I sat next to him and folded my hands in my lap. "I'm ready whenever you are."

He tipped his head down as if the fabric on the chair was the most important thing he needed to see. I wasn't about to push him to open up. After my family's book of witchcraft clonked me on the head almost a year ago and I discovered my rescue cat could talk, I learned patience was the key to good communication with Milo.

"Have you ever wondered how I became a familiar?"

His normal snarky kitty growl was absent, and he sounded as if he had lost his only friend. I knew I was about to say something stupid, but I had to ask. "You weren't born a familiar?"

He lifted his head and glared at me. "Familiars aren't born. We're made from other beings such as a witch or wizard."

"Oh." What was I expected to say and how would I have known? Should I have thought to ask when I learned the truth about myself and him? "What were you, a witch?"

His nod was barely noticeable. As he began to speak, I leaned closer so as not to miss a single word. "It was a long time ago, and I was respected as a fair and honorable witch. But some craved the power I possessed. You see, as a young witch, I discovered the rarest red opal anyone had ever seen. I had crafted an amulet and imbued it with a spell that as long as I wore it, my powers would remain pure and strong. As the years went by, I grew complacent. I let my guard down. A witch joined our coven in the neighboring village. There were whispers, but I let arrogance cloud my judgement. She wanted to claim the amulet I wore around my neck for herself. With trickery, she got my amulet and cursed me to life as a familiar. Before her spell changed the course of my life, I was able to change the course of hers. I cursed the amulet that whoever should wear it, if they had an impure heart, would perish."

My hand flew to my mouth. "Milo, you cast a death curse?"

"Yes, and you deserve to know the truth before I leave. I did the unforgivable."

"Did the witch who took your amulet..." I didn't want to say the words, and thank the stars Milo didn't wait for me to finish my question.

"Yes. She died. It was such a chaotic time in our town. The power struggles between good witches and evil. A tale as old as time. There were rumors, of course, about the amulet, but I lost track of it. Now, this beautiful, cursed object is part of a traveling exhibit and should never fall into the wrong hands." He lay down and covered his head with his paws in shame.

Why was he telling me this now? And I quickly rewound the events from earlier. "Milo."

When he didn't pick his head up, I scooped him from

the chair. After placing a tender kiss on the middle of his head and holding him away from my body so I could see into his deep green eyes. "Milo, what was the name of your amulet?" My heart thudded in my chest. I knew before he would tell me, but I had to hear it from him.

"The amulet of Aathmika."

"And you're Aathmika." There was no need for the question. I just needed confirmation. "What does that mean?"

"Once upon a time, I was. It means soulful and close to the inner heart." He hung his head. "Now, instead of being a powerful witch, I am a humble teacher for you, my dear witch."

I crushed him to my chest and blinked the tears from my eyes. "Your amulet is in our library."

"Yes, and I can tell you that woman who was here plans to steal it."

"Petra Addington? How do you know that?"

"Guess." He squirmed from my arms and dropped to the floor. "I followed them and heard what they were saying. Non-magical people never pay attention to a cat when they're talking." He ran his paw over one side of his whiskers. "For the record, Simon was still arguing with her. He said she was being foolish. There was no way she would get her hands on it." He grumbled, "Heart of the Soul. You have to ask yourself who renamed that to make it sound sweet and innocent."

"Well, it's based on facts. You said it means soul and inner heart. At some point, the name was changed." I got to my feet. "I texted Gage, and we're meeting at the library. Do you want to come with us or stay here?"

Milo's body shook from the tips of his whiskers to the end of his tail. "I don't know that I want to see it. After all this time, it still might be too painful. A reminder of all that I've lost."

I knelt on the floor and ran my hand over the length of his soft fur. "Milo, you won't be alone. I'll be with you. And whatever happened all those years ago can't hurt you again."

He leaned into my hand. "Lily, you'll need to do some recon work and confirm the curse is still as strong as ever. The amulet must be protected at all costs. If it falls into the wrong hands, I shudder to think what might happen, especially if it's a non-magical. That screams disaster."

"How can I do that short of putting the amulet on? Which, for the record, I don't even want to think about doing. Should I have Dax come with Gage?"

"First, you're a Michaels witch and pure of heart. I don't think it could hurt you." Milo nodded when I mentioned a more seasoned witch to accompany us. Gage was a non-magical, and I was still new at a lot of witchy stuff.

"Asking Detective Sweet Tea to join us might not be a bad idea. Dax Peters is more than competent; his powers are off the charts. But why don't you ask them to come by here first, and I can fill them in on the high-level curse information? I wouldn't want your Detective Cutie to try and touch it. There's no way to know just how strong the magic is."

I loved that Milo had given them both nicknames. Gage was really good looking, and Dax, being from Louisiana, got the moniker, Sweet Tea, not that he drank much tea; coffee was his beverage of choice. But the names were endearing. I had one lingering question. "Where did you get the name Milo?"

"My familiar gave his life protecting me. It was the best way I knew to honor his sacrifice."

A lump rose in my throat. I made a silent vow. Never

put my precious Milo in a position where he'd have to protect me at the cost of putting his own life in peril. I pulled him to my chest and smothered him with kisses.

"Stop." He swatted my cheek with his paw, claw tucked in. He coughed like he wanted to hack up a small hairball. "Now, what about reading some of the book *Practical Beginnings?* You never know when you might need a new spell."

I gave him a half smile. "Are you kidding I'm going to start at the beginning and read every single page. If trouble is brewing, I'm going to be prepared."

"First text Gage, and don't forget to ask Detective Sweet Tea to come too." He slipped from my arms and stalked to the window seat. "I need a nap."

He turned around three times and curled into a ball. So much had happened in the last fifteen minutes, I felt like I'd been sideswiped with information. My familiar once had been a powerful witch. Didn't my aunt Mimi know, and if she did, why in the heavens and earth hadn't she told me? First things first, text Gage. Then, call my aunt.

Artifacts & Amulets
A Book Store Cozy Mystery Series
Order Now

Or
Shop at Lucinda Race

A Free Story for You

Have you enjoyed Magicians & Murder? Not ready to stop reading yet? If you sign up for my newsletter at www.lucin darace.com/newsletter, you will receive Cookies & Capers, which is the start of Lily and Milo's adventure, as my thank-you gift for choosing to get my newsletter.

Cookies & Capers

I stood in front of the old wood and glass door as I pocketed the keys to the Cozy Nook Bookshop. A few weeks ago Aunt Mimi had signed her bookstore over to me. She said it felt like giving me her baby. But I loved the shop as much as my aunt did. We had worked together for the last twelve years. I had attended the University of Maine and majored in history. I had always wanted to be a teacher, but jobs were scarce, and after substituting for a few years, I moved back to my hometown of Pembroke Cove Maine. And Aunt Mimi hired me as soon as my suitcase was unpacked.

Spending time with my aunt learning the business had been the best experience. I offered to buy the business when she wanted to retire, but she wouldn't hear of it. As long as she had free books for life, and her long-term boyfriend Nate, she said it was a fair deal. From my point of view, I had built-in backup for years to come.

Now that I was the bookshop owner, Aunt Mimi was no longer coming in every day which meant her cat, Phoenix, wasn't either. The space felt empty without a kitty lying in the window or skulking about as kitties do. I was off to the Pembroke Animal Palace to see if I could find a match.

It was a short walk in the bright noonday sun. The spring air from the ocean carried a tang of salt, but the breeze was refreshing. I waved to one of my best friends, Gage Erikson, as he drove past in his police-issued sedan. My heart fluttered in my chest.

He was a detective on the force. Not that we had much crime in our small seaside town. But one of these days, I was going to get brave and confess that I had been carrying a torch for him since we were in ninth grade. What's the worst thing that could happen? We'd still be best friends, right?

I continued down the sidewalk waving to William from the Sweet Spot Bakery. He was sweeping the sidewalk wearing a large pristine white apron and a wide smile. A deep inhale confirmed my suspicion, he was baking cookies. My mouth watered. I did a half turn and went back to where he was finishing up. "Hello, William." I bobbed my head in the direction of the shop. "What is that tantalizing smell?"

He held open the brightly polished glass door. "One of your favorites, Lily. Chocolate chip and pecan cookies. Can I interest you in one before you continue on your mission?"

I gave him a sidelong look. "Mission?"

He chuckled. "Over the years, my Lulu would say you

had two speeds, strolling and purposeful. Just now, it was your purposeful speed, so hence, you're on a mission."

"I'm going to the shelter in hopes of finding a kitty. The shop is lonely now that Phoenix is home every day with Aunt Mimi. I feel a cat napping in the window adds an air of serenity to the place."

"Unless you're allergic."

He had a point but, not willing to be deterred, I smiled. "I'm always happy to deliver to a customer if that's the case." I leaned over the glass bakery case, like a kid pressing her nose against the candy case. "You made sugar cookies too and frosted them?" I sighed. I was going to need to exercise more if he continued to bake all my favorites. I looked up, and he was smiling at me like an indulgent grandfather. "Are the chocolate pecan ready?"

He wiggled his eyebrows. "I have a tray cooling in the back."

"Then can I have one of those and a sugar cookie, but to go."

With a flick of his wrist, he snapped open a white bakery bag and called over his shoulder. "Jerilyn, would you please bring out the last batch of cookies?"

I heard a muffled, "Coming," and smiled. "I'm glad Jerilyn stayed on." I didn't say anything about his beloved wife Lulu passing away. It was too painful for us all.

He nodded. "Me too. She's a hard worker and is excellent with customers."

Jerilyn bustled in from the back room carrying a large stainless steel tray. It was lined with parchment paper and cookies the size of the palm of my hand. It was going to taste so good later with a hot cup of tea.

William slipped two in the bag along with two sugar cookies. He handed the bag to me. I paid for my cookies and thanked him. "Stop by the shop later. You might just get to meet my new fur baby."

"Sounds like a plan." He grinned and crossed his arms over his rounded midsection. "You're more like your aunt than you realize. Ever since she opened that bookshop, she's had a cat too."

I paused, tucked the bakery bag in my tote, and with my hand on the door, I gave him a wide grin. "And now it's time I carry on the tradition." With a jaunty wave, I called, "Wish me luck."

I reached the old, cedar-shingled building with a bright blue door, it had been many businesses over the course of its life. Now it was occupied by the animal shelter. I considered what kind of a cat I'd want. An older cat, that was all cuddly and would want to snuggle at night while I was reading a good book or watching old movies. Or would a younger kitten be a better choice so that our chances of having many years together would be optimal? Would there even be a cat that I'd connect with? This wasn't the first time I had tried to adopt one. Each time it just didn't feel right. Or maybe I wasn't ready at the time.

I marched up the granite steps, and the heavy wood door swung open with ease. I stepped inside and noticed the smell of pine cleaner tickled my nose. The lobby was empty except for a young woman sitting behind the desk. I approached it and smiled at her.

"Hello. I'm Lily Michaels, and I'd like to see cats that are available for adoption."

The young lady lifted her head and pulled her earbuds out. With a shy smile she said, "I'm sorry. What did you say? I was listening to a lecture from one of my classes."

I wasn't upset she hadn't heard me, but it was nice to

know she was doing something so worthwhile. "What are you studying?"

She perked up. "I'm going to be a doctor. A vet." With a blush, she said, "I'm here to do an internship for the summer." She stuck out her hand. "Judy Blume. And yes, my mom's favorite book was written by Judy Blume."

"It's very nice to meet you, and welcome to Pembroke Cove. I hope you enjoy the summer here. There's nothing like the Cove in June." I leaned forward. "As long as the weather holds. It can be chilly."

"Thanks for the intel. How can I help you?" She snapped her fingers and bobbed her head. "Wait. You said you wanted to see our cats." She whisked the chair back and grinned. "Don't you just love chairs on wheels?"

Her bright and cheery outlook could put a smile on anyone's face. "They certainly come in handy." I followed through the pale blue door behind the desk.

"We'll go right into the cat room. There are a few others that just came in so they're waiting for a vet check before we mix them with the others. But I can show you those too."

We entered a good-size room. Scattered about were scratching posts, a few kitty condos where several cats were lounging, and lots of toys.

"They've all been spayed or neutered, so after a quick check on you and your landlord, we can send one home with you."

"I own my house so no landlord to call." I moved slowly around the room. I crouched down to scratch behind ears but so far not one kitty looked up with an inquisitive gaze to meet mine. Again, no connection but they were all so darn cute. I realized I really did want to find a fur-ever friend.

Judy was giving me space to interact with the cats, and

after picking a couple up, there was no zip. I gave her a look that I'm sure expressed my disappointment.

"How about we try the room next door?"

We went into the room next to the first one, and it was much of the same. I picked up a black cat which reminded me of Phoenix, but there was only one in our family. I gave him a kiss on the head and put him down too. "I guess I'll have to come back another day."

Judy snapped her fingers, and if I had to guess, she did that often. "There's a gray tabby that was picked up yesterday. He's in an isolation room waiting for the vet. Poor baby. He's in great shape, but he was found just wandering around, and he isn't microchipped. The director thinks he's a stray since he's never seen him around before." She opened the door. "Wait until you see him, he's a very handsome little dude."

Intrigued, I followed her into a small examination room. Sitting on the side chair was a gray tabby cat with a long tail, and Judy had been right. He was adorable. His eyes locked on mine, and he watched me closely as I crossed the short distance between us. I picked him up and held him close to my chest. Instantly, he began to purr a low comforting sound, and he tucked his head under my chin. Tears sprang to my eyes. This was my kitty.

Judy said quietly. "I'm going to leave you two so you can get better acquainted." She slipped from the room, and I placed him on the chair and dropped to the floor. Under the chair was a little mouse. I could smell the faint aroma of mint. Catnip.

"Hey little man. Do you want to play?"

The cat tipped his head and stared at me. Instead of tossing the mouse, I stretched out my legs and patted my lap. "Come sit with me."

He dropped graciously to the floor and crept closer, taking his own sweet time. He turned around once, twice, and a third time before finally settling on my lap. He tucked his front paws under his chest, and his eyes closed to mere slits. And once again he began that soft low purr. That's when I knew I we were a bonded pair.

As I scratched his head I said, "What should I call you. That is if you want to come home with me."

He rolled over on his back and put his paws up in the air exposing his belly. I laughed. "I'll take that as a yes?" We sat there for several minutes. The cat purring and me trying to come up with a name.

"What should I call you?"

The cat stopped purring and flipped over to a sitting position. He looked me directly in the eye. Instantly I knew. His name was Milo.

It took three days for Milo and me to become a little family. The minute I carried the cat carrier in the house and set it down, he put his paw on the metal door and meowed very loudly. He wanted out!

I was going to let him explore to his heart's content while I set up his food and water bowls. When I finished, I turned around and saw him staring at me from the kitchen table. I picked him up and set him on the tile floor. "Go explore your new home."

He tipped his head, and I wondered if he was nervous. There was no way to tell what he had gone through before being taken to the shelter. I opened the bag of salmon treats and gave him one. He took it delicately from my fingers.

"All right. I'll give you the grand tour. I hope you like it here." I walked from the kitchen into the living room and pointed to the sofa and recliner. "No scratching the furniture. Got it?"

He tipped his head to the side and blinked.

"I'm going to take that as a yes." I walked from room to room showing him the office and my bedroom. In the window seat, I sat down and patted a small cushion. "I thought you might like to snooze here."

Milo hopped up and looked out the window before settling down. "I'm going to take that as it's kitty approved."

Cookies & Capers is only available by signing up for my newsletter – sign up for it here at <u>www.lucindarace.com/ newsletter</u>

Love to read?

**All ebooks and signed paperback copies can be
ordered from my website at:
Shop at Lucinda Race**

Cozy Mystery Books
A Bookstore Cozy Mystery Series 2023
***Welcome to Pembroke Cove, where witches and
murders are multiplying…***
Books & Bribes
*It was an ordinary day until the book of Practical Magic
conked Lily on the head causing her to see stars. And then
she discovered her cat, Milo, could talk.*

Catnaps & Crimes
A witch, a snarky familiar and murder…

Tea & Trouble
*When reading tea leaves turns to murder can Lily solve this
latest case?*

Love to read?

Scares & Dares
What does a haunted house and murder have in common?
New witch Lily Michaels is determined to solve the case.

Holidays & Homicide
Even a fun event like the annual Glow & Glide can lose its
charm when a body is discovered on the ice.

Leprechauns & Larceny
A leprechaun, a wedding, and pirate treasure, Oh My!

Magicians & Murder
When four magicians roll into town for a show more than
fun is on one person's mind.

Artifacts & Amulets August 2024
Milo has been keeping secrets, which can be deadly.

Cranberries & Criminals November 2024

Cowboys of River Junction

Second Chances in Montana
*Twenty years later Renee and Hank are back where they fell
in love, but reality is like a spring frost and is a long-distance
relationship their only option for their second chance?*

Stars Over Montana
*The cowboy broke her heart but he never stopped loving her.
Now she's back ready to run her grandfather's ranch...*

Hiding in Montana
Can love flourish while danger lurks in the shadow?

Love to read?

Moonlight Over Montana
Will a single mom find love with the handsome cowboy who saved her and her daughter from danger?

The Sandy Bay Series
<u>Sundaes on Sunday</u>
A widowed school teacher and the airline pilot whose little girl is determined to bring her daddy and the lady from the ice cream shop together for a second chance at love.

Last Man Standing/Always a Bridesmaid
<u>Barrett</u>
Has the last man standing finally met his match?

<u>Marie</u>
Career focused city girl discovers small town charm can lead to love.

Price Family Series
<u>Breathe</u>
Her dream come true may be the end of his...
Crush
The first time they met was fleeting, the second time restarted her heart.
<u>Blush</u>
He's always loved her, but he left. Now he's back...the question, does she still love him?
<u>Vintage</u>
He's an unexpected distraction, she gets his engine running...
<u>Bouquet</u>
Sweet second chances for a widow and the handsome billionaire...

Holiday Romance

Love to read?

<u>The Sugar Plum Inn</u>
The chef and the restaurant critic are about to come face to face.
Last Chance Beach
<u>Shamrocks are a Girl's Best Friend</u>
Will a bit of Irish luck and a matchmaking uncle give Kelly and Tric a chance to find love?

A Dickens Holiday Romance
<u>Holiday Heart Wishes</u>
Heartfelt wishes and holiday kisses...

<u>Holly Berries and Hockey Pucks</u>
Hockey, holidays, and a slap shot to the heart.

<u>Christmas in July</u>
She's the hometown girl with the hometown advantage. Right?

<u>A Secret Santa Christmas</u>
Christmas isn't Holly's thing, but will a family secret help her find the true meaning of Christmas?

It's Just Coffee Series
<u>The Matchmaker and The Marine</u>
She vowed never to love again. His career in the Marines crushed his ability to love. Can undeniable chemistry and a leap of faith overcome their past?

The MacLellan Sisters Trilogy
<u>Old and New</u>
An enchanted heirloom wedding dress and a letter change

Social Media

Follow Me on Social Media

Like my Facebook page
Join Lucinda's Heart Racer's Reader Group on Facebook
Twitter @lucindarace
Instagram @lucindraceauthor
BookBub
Goodreads
Pinterest

About the Author

Award-winning and best-selling author Lucinda Race is a lifelong fan of reading. As a young girl, she spent hours reading novels and getting lost in the fun and hope they represent. While her friends dreamed of becoming doctors and engineers, her dream was to become a writer—a novelist.

As life twisted and turned, she found herself writing nonfiction but longed to turn to her true passion. After developing the storyline for A McKenna Family Romance, it was time to start living her dream. Her fingers practically fly over computer keys as she weaves stories of mystery and romance.

Lucinda lives with her two little dogs, a miniature long-haired dachshund and a shih tzu mix rescue, in the rolling hills of western Massachusetts. When she's not at her day job, she's immersed in her fictional worlds. And if she's not writing romance or cozy mystery novels, she's reading everything she can get her hands on.

www.ingramcontent.com/pod-product-compliance
Lightning Source LLC
Chambersburg PA
CBHW061258210726
48293CB00003B/1021